JESSICA BECK

THE DONUT MYSTERIES, BOOK 21

CRIMINAL CRUMBS

The First Time Ever Published!

The 21st Donut Mystery.

Jessica Beck is the *New York Times* Bestselling Author of the Donut Mysteries, the Classic Diner Mysteries, the Ghost Cat Cozy Mysteries, and the Cast Iron Cooking Mysteries.

To Kath and Tom,
Family in every way that counts!!

When Suzanne accepts Grace's invitation to a luxurious corporate weekend retreat, she believes she's in for some first class pampering, but when one of the participants dies soon after they arrive, she's thrown back into the world of detecting, whether she likes it or not. To make matters worse, they are soon cut off from the rest of the world, and the group finds itself trapped on a mountaintop with a cold blooded killer.

FOREWORD

THIS BOOK WAS INSPIRED BY a recent visit to the Mountain Lake Lodge in Penbroke, Virginia, better known as the site where much of the movie *Dirty Dancing* was filmed. In *Bad Bites*, an earlier donut mystery, Jake and Suzanne visit a lodge in the latter stages of the book, but by no means does the entirety of that mystery take place there. I decided that it might be fun to revisit a different lodge setting as a backdrop for this donut murder mystery, since there are so many lodges in my part of North Carolina and Virginia. It's not unreasonable, at least in my mind, to assume that Suzanne would visit more than one lodge in her lifetime, but I wanted to make you, my dear reader, aware that I'm not repeating myself with this entry; rather, I'm exploring more of a particular favorite vacation setting of mine. And honestly, we must let the denizens of April Springs be excused from a murder now and then, or the town will soon be decimated.

For those of you have enjoyed the Donut Mysteries, along with my other series in the cozy mystery world (insert blatant plug for the Classic Diner mysteries, the Cast Iron Mysteries, and the Ghost Cat mysteries here), I thank you.

I'll be waiting on the other side, working on the next adventure we can share together.

The Author

CHAPTER 1

T HOUGH IT WAS JUST A little past nine on a late autumn evening, I was sick with worry. Where was my best friend, Grace, and why hadn't she returned to the cottage in the woods we were sharing for the long weekend? Had something happened to her on her solo walk back from the main lodge? I peered out the window searching for her in the darkness, but the glass might as well have been painted jet black for all the good it did me. Saying that it was dark outside couldn't begin to describe the complete and utter absence of light I found. This wasn't anything like the wee hours back in April Springs when I left the house in the middle of the night to get ready for my day at Donut Hearts making treats for my fellow townsfolk. Although those short trips were nominally nighttime, there were always lots of little lights here and there along the way, ambient illumination emanating from the small town where I lived and worked that offered beacons beyond the scope of my Jeep's headlights. Not this—it was a dense, woodsy dark, one devoid of all extraneous light, where only the hope of an exposed moon could guide steps. Only there was no moon tonight, at least not one that I could see. Our guest cottage, scattered among three others just like it, was perched along a narrow path that skirted a dramatically steep drop-off on one side, and while it felt perfectly safe coming and going in the light of day, at night, it was another matter altogether. Was Grace lingering over coffee while sitting in one of the comfortable couches that surrounded the massive stone fireplace at the lodge, talking to one of the women she worked with at her cosmetics company, trading war stories of nightmare bosses and clients they'd endured over their years of service? Or was her fate something far more sinister? Could she have strayed from the unlit path and plummeted into the forest below, even now lying there in pain, calling out for me?

She should have been back twenty minutes earlier, and I knew that I never should have let her stay back at the lodge without me. I'd been sleepy, used to my odd nocturnal habit of going to bed around seven, and Grace had caught me yawning before sending me off to enjoy my rest. But that had turned out to be impossible after all. The night air had been too bracing on my walk back, sending chilled fingers through the hooded sweatshirt and heavy jeans I'd had on. We were in true mountains, at twice the elevation of April Springs, and when we'd left home, it had been just over seventy degrees. Now, just seven hours later, the thermometer was hovering somewhere around forty, and if the temperature at the moment was any indication, it would get colder still before morning came. I paced around inside the small stone cottage, wondering what I should do, until I finally decided to just face the cold and go out in search of her. Chances were good that I'd find her safe in the lodge, wondering what had brought me out again, but I didn't care if I looked foolish showing up again unexpectedly.

I had to make sure that she was safe.

Grabbing the flashlight they'd issued me upon checking in, I walked out into the cold night, bracing myself for the wind and the oppressive darkness. Turning on my light as I stepped outside, I kept it to the gravel path in front of me as I made my way to the lodge. Glancing up at the sky, I could see wave upon wave of dark clouds overhead. If it had been a clear night, I was certain that the stars would have been breathtaking, but there was nothing but shadows of gray above me. Maybe that was why they'd called the place Shadow Mountain Resort so long ago.

I was halfway to the lodge when I heard the first scream, so close that I could almost touch it, and I nearly plummeted over the path's edge as I raced toward it.

And then a second, higher-pitched scream filled the night air again.

Someone was clearly in trouble.

I just hoped and prayed that it wasn't Grace as I ran in the direction of the sound I'd just heard piercing the night.

Whatever had just happened, I knew in my heart that it had spelled disaster for someone in our weekend group.

CHAPTER 2

Two days earlier.

"Hey, Suzanne," Grace said when she walked into my donut shop a little before closing one day. "Please tell me that you have an apple fritter left for me." It wasn't unusual to see my best friend at my shop, especially after she'd decided to forgo depriving herself of the treats and goodies I sold at Donut Hearts and indulge along with the rest of us. Once upon a time she'd insisted on gluten-free, fat-free, sugar-free fare, but these days she'd been known to enjoy an apple fritter and a cup of coffee with the best of them. I was a fan of fritters myself, made from dough too overworked for any other kind of treat. They were dense and rich like no other, and I delighted in embedding the dough with tiny bits of apple and cinnamon before I fried them and then coated them heavily with the thick icing I poured over most of my other donuts. Somehow the sweet coating tasted different on the fritters, perhaps because of all of the nooks and crannies that could hold more icing than a plain round shape could.

"You're in luck. I have two left," I said as I grabbed one for her.

"Since you have two, would you care to join me?" she asked me with a grin.

Usually I tried to abstain from eating too much of what I made and sold. After all, if I sampled just one thing every day,

I'd soon have trouble getting through the door, and though my husband, Jake, said that he liked my curves, I wanted to be sure that I didn't get completely round. Then again, what would one hurt? "Why not?"

The shop was nearly empty, and it was close enough to the end of my working day, though it was still not quite eleven o'clock in the morning, that I felt comfortable shutting down early. We had less than a dozen donuts left for sale anyway, and Grace and I were about to wipe out two of those. I flipped the sign, locked the door, and then I served us by one of the couches near the window.

As I placed the fritters and coffees on the table, I studied Grace a little more closely. "Why are you grinning like that? Did something happen with Stephen?" She'd been dating Officer Stephen Grant for some time, and I was happy that the fact that he was working for my husband, if only temporarily, hadn't interfered with our friendship. Jake was retired from the state police, but my friend the mayor had asked him to step in when we'd had a sudden vacancy as police chief, and Jake had acquiesced. The truth was George hadn't had to twist his arm all that much. I had a feeling that Jake missed being an officer of the law, no matter how much he protested to the contrary.

"No, everything's fine and dandy. We're still getting along splendidly, so there are no changes to report on that front," she said. "This isn't about him. It's about us."

"Us?" I asked. "What do you mean?"

"Suzanne, how would you like an all-expenses-paid trip to Shadow Mountain Resort? It's for three glorious days, and it won't cost you a dime."

I'd read about the resort before, a getaway in the mountains where, in the twenties and thirties, movie stars and business magnates had gone to escape the heat, living in opulence and enjoying all the comforts their money and fame could afford them. It was an exciting prospect, but then I realized that I'd have to refuse it nonetheless. "As much as I'd love to, we just can't do it. Jake's shorthanded right now. He's even doing some of the patrol routes at night himself. I'm really sorry."

Grace wasn't finished yet, though. "Funny, but I don't remember inviting him. I thought I just asked you to go with me."

"Oh. Sorry. That was presumptuous of me, wasn't it?" I asked her with a grin.

"Suzanne, I know how busy our men are. No offense, but I asked Stephen first. When he declined, I immediately thought of you. Just because the fellows in our lives are busy keeping April Springs safe doesn't mean that we can't have a girls' weekend away, does it? And don't tell me that you can't get away from this place," she added as she waved a hand around Donut Hearts. "I know that Emma and her mother would be perfectly happy to step in and take over for you for three days." She took my hands in hers, setting her fritter aside for a moment. "Suzanne, the truth is, I miss you. Before Jake came into your life and Stephen came into mine, we used to spend most of our free time together. Remember how it was after your divorce from Max?"

It was true. I'd fallen apart after finding my husband with another woman, and two people had gotten me through those dark days: Grace and my mother. Momma had taken me in, and Grace had helped me put my life back together as I'd started over. I'd bought Donut Hearts on a whim and ended up changing the course of my life forever. "I remember," I said.

"Come on. It will be fun. We're having a district retreat, and we're each allowed to bring one guest. What do you say? It will be great."

"Isn't it a little late in the season to be visiting a mountain resort?" I asked her.

"Why do you think we're having our retreat there then? It's probably too expensive during the summer. We're booking the entire place, and they've agreed to stay open for us, even though their official closing was last weekend. Come on. What do you say?"

The idea of having some time away with Grace sounded wonderful, and the setting didn't hurt, either. It was probably the only way I'd ever be able to afford to go there, given how much it would have cost Jake and me to visit it. I'd miss him, but it was only for three days, and with our schedules lately, I wasn't sure how much time together we'd actually miss. "Let me talk to Jake and Sharon first, and I'll let you know. When is the retreat?"

"It's in two days," she said with a grin.

"Wow, not much notice, is it?"

"Hey, just be glad you're getting invited at all," she said. "No rush, but could you check with them both now?"

"Why, so you can line someone else up to take my place if I can't make it?" I asked her with a smile.

"Nope, that's not it at all. I have to tell my boss who I'm bringing," she said. "Go on. Check with everybody. I can wait." Grace had finished her fritter, and she was now eyeing mine.

"I'll be right back," I said, taking my fritter with me. I trusted Grace with my life, but my fritter? No, I didn't think so.

"Hey, Jake. Do you have a second?" I asked him when he picked up.

Before I could say another word, he broke in. "I think you should go, Suzanne. You and Grace don't spend nearly enough time together, and besides, you know how busy I'm going to be."

"Did she already talk to you about it?" I asked him.

"No, but Grant and I are making our rounds together, and it came up in conversation that he'd turned Grace down. I didn't need to know anything else to realize that you'd be her next choice. So go. Have fun. Just not too much fun, okay?"

I grinned, and I knew that it would be in my voice. "Just exactly how much fun is too much?"

"If you need bail money, then you've probably gone a little bit too far. For anything less than that, go on and knock yourself out."

"Jake, you're not trying to get rid of me, are you? This has all been just a little too easy. There aren't any cuties in town you have your eye on, are there?"

His laugh was full and rich. "You're kidding, right? I can't keep up with the woman I have. Why on earth would I want to complicate my life any more than it already is?"

"I love you, too," I said happily.

"Right back at you."

After I hung up with Jake, I turned to Grace. "One down, one to go."

Sharon was equally enthusiastic. She used her occasional stints filling in for me for travel money, and she had a big trip planned if she could find a way to finance it. It looked as though everything was set. Grace and I were going to go to Shadow Mountain Resort, and hopefully, we'd have a memorable experience together.

It turned out to be exactly that, all right, and much, much more.

Grace drove us in her newest company car, a luxury vehicle I could have never afforded on my donutmaking income, not that I didn't love my Jeep, even if it was getting older and more temperamental by the minute. "So, how are you doing? Really?" Grace asked me three quarters of the way through our journey as we neared the place where a steep ascent began that eventually led to our weekend getaway on the mountaintop.

"I'm doing fine."

She took her gaze off the road for a second and looked steadily at me. "I mean really, truly, honestly."

It was something we'd said to each other as kids when only the unvarnished truth would do. "I'm great. The business is doing well, my marriage is wonderful, and Momma and I have never gotten along better. Why do you ask?"

"I don't know," she said with a sigh. "Suzanne, there's a sadness about you these days that I haven't seen in a long time. It's not there all of the time, but I still see it enough to worry about you."

"Is that why you really asked me along on this trip?" I asked her. "You should turn around and take me home if that's it. I'm fine. I'll see if Jake will let Stephen off for three days."

"I want to spend this time with *you*," she insisted. "Don't be so touchy. You know as well as I do that you're still having a hard time with what happened on that roof. There's no use trying to deny it."

I'd hoped that wasn't what she'd meant, but clearly it was. It was true. I wished that I could refute it, but I couldn't. A life had been lost directly because of my actions, even though the killer had died trying to end me once and forever. That still hadn't made the outcome any easier to accept. I'd been in a fog for several weeks, but I thought I'd finally snapped out of it. Maybe I was wrong, though, if Grace could still see the overwhelming sadness in me. "Jake and I have talked it out. There was nothing I could do. It's horrible that it happened, but in the end, I'm glad that it wasn't me going off that roof. Am I sad and upset that it happened? Of course I am. Is it going to ruin the rest of my life? Not a chance. I think about it less and less every day, and I imagine, or should I say that I hope, that someday I won't think about it at all. That's the best answer that I can give you right now."

She reached over and patted my leg. "That's all I need. I suppose the main question lurking in the dark recesses of my mind is if you are sure that our crime-solving days together are really over?" Grace asked it with a grin, and I tried to return it with one of my own, though it felt feeble to me even as I was doing it.

"I've learned never to say never, but as of right now, I'm retired, now and forever," I said.

"Okay. I thought I'd ask, just in case."

"Is there something specific you had in mind, Grace?"

I stared at her without saying another word, and I watched as she grew more and more uncomfortable with the attention, until she finally found a shoulder off the side of the road and pulled over. "Suzanne, there's something I haven't told you yet. You should know up front that I want your company, first and foremost, this weekend, and if you don't want to get involved, that's fine by me, but I've committed to it, so I'm going to do what I can, with or without your help."

"Grace, what have you gotten yourself into?"

"It's a long story," she said.

"Then pull back onto the road and start driving. We have a thirty-minute drive up the mountain. Can you tell it to me in that amount of time?"

"I should be able to," she said.

"Then if you can talk and drive at the same time, tell me what's going on."

"Somebody's trying to kill my new boss," she said flatly.

I was glad that I wasn't the one driving.

I wasn't sure that I would have been able to keep my car on the road.

"Are you serious?"

"Never more in my life," Grace said grimly.

"What makes her think someone wants her dead?" I couldn't help myself. Though I'd sworn off amateur detective work, this was different. In the first place, no one had been murdered, at least not yet. In the second, I was as far removed from the victim as I could possibly be. We hadn't even met! But third, and most important of all, Grace needed my help. How could I say no to her, given what we meant to each other?

"Are you sure you want to hear this?"

"I'm not letting you do this alone. If I can help, you can count on me."

She reached over for a moment and patted my arm. "Thanks, Suzanne. I'll admit that I wasn't crazy about doing this without you."

"Start from the beginning, okay?" I asked her.

"I'll tell you what I know. If there's anything else, we'll have to get it from Nicole. That's her name, by the way, Nicole Thurman. She came up through the ranks with me, and when our old boss got promoted, the district manager thought it would be fun to have a competition to see who got the job."

"What did you do, arm wrestle for it?" I asked.

"That might have been simpler. No, he set impossible goals, made it ridiculously easy to cheat, and then he stood back and watched the bloodbath."

"Why didn't I hear anything about this from you?" I asked her. Normally Grace shared quite a bit with me, and while I knew that I'd been spending an inordinate amount of time with my husband lately, there had still been opportunities for the two of us to talk about what was going on in Grace's life. Or had there been as many as I thought?

"The truth is, I didn't want to bother you with it," she said, averting her gaze.

"Listen to me carefully, Grace Gauge. I'm not a delicate flower. You don't have to tiptoe around me."

"Any more, you mean?" she asked me with the hint of a smile.

"Was I really that bad?" I asked her.

"Suzanne, you were in pain. We all made an effort not to bring your spirits down any lower than they already were. Besides, it wasn't as though the job was important to me. I've given up promotions in the past so I could stay in April Springs, remember? I've found my perfect spot in the world. Why would I want to give that up? For more money? I've got everything I need and more, thank you very much. The prestige of being higher up on the corporate ladder? No, I don't think so. I was happy for Nicole when she got the job, especially because she earned it."

"I thought you said the system was set up for cheating. Are you certain that she came by it fair and square?"

Grace glanced over at me, and I could see a grin forming. "That's where the district manager was really devious. I said it was easy to cheat, but it was also fairly simple to discover who had played by the rules and who tried to lie their way into the position. Two of our other reps were caught trying to game the system. Not only were they disqualified from the promotion, but they were both put on probation. Of the remaining contenders, Nicole was the obvious winner."

"How did the two cheaters get caught?" I asked her.

"Nicole came up with a way to verify that their reports were completely fabricated, and she took it to the district manager," Grace said uncomfortably. "I probably would have done the same thing if I'd wanted that job for myself. Word got out, though, and the resentment is still pretty obvious."

"Would someone actually kill their boss over a promotion?" I asked her. In my donut world, I was already at the top. Emma, my young assistant, was my only other employee, and I couldn't imagine the circumstances that would make her do something to me to try to take over Donut Hearts.

"You've lived a sheltered life, Suzanne. This was a very big deal, a career builder or breaker. Nicole likes expensive things, from designer dresses to elegant jewelry. Getting that promotion allowed her to feed what must be a pretty expensive habit by now."

"Hang on a second," I said. "Before you tell me more about your list of suspects, what makes Nicole believe that someone is trying to kill her?"

"I asked her the same thing when she started telling me about this a few days ago," Grace said. "At first she thought she was just being paranoid, but as events started to escalate, she decided to come to me with her concerns. You and I have a bit of a reputation, did you know that? It appears that our efforts at catching killers in the past haven't gone unnoticed. But you asked me about specific incidents. The first one happened while she was out jogging one morning before work. It was dark out, and she was listening to an audiobook on her headphones, so she didn't hear the car coming. In fact, if she hadn't looked up at precisely the right moment, she said that she would have been run over. Nicole managed to jump into the bushes nearby, but she didn't catch sight of who did it."

"Couldn't that have been an unrelated accident?"

"She was certain that the intent was there. Why else would someone drive in the dark with no headlights on and then swerve to hit her at exactly the right moment? Nicole tried to put it out of her mind, and then her house almost blew up."

CHAPTER 3

"WHAT!"

"She had a reception at her home for all of us, including her family, to celebrate her promotion. After everyone left, she went to bed, but something made her uneasy. She checked her place from top to bottom, and she discovered that someone had blown out her pilot light in her hot water heater. She would have either been asphyxiated or blown up if there'd been a spark to set it off. She even had one of those all-purpose detectors in the utility room, but the batteries in it had been reversed, making it useless as anything but a paperweight."

"Why didn't she call the police when it happened?"

"She thought about it, but then she realized how it would appear to someone from the outside. Unfortunately, cars hit pedestrians much too often, especially when it's dark, and pilot lights blow out on occasion. As for the detector, it could be explained as an unfortunate accident that she'd replaced the batteries incorrectly. Nicole knows that someone's out to get her, though, and she asked me to help her find out who's after her."

"Okay, she's got reason enough to be concerned," I said. "Who makes up her list of suspects?"

"The two women we work with who are now on probation because of her, Janelle Best and Georgia Collier, to start with. If you ask me, either woman might be capable of trying to kill Nicole for her job. Janelle is a single mom, not that she sees her kids all that much. She's constantly trying to claw her way to the top. Oh, and she's a petty thief, too."

"What does she steal, cosmetics?" I asked.

"As far as I've been able to tell, there's only one criterion—it has to be of little enough value for the owner not to be too upset by its absence. I'm talking about things like office supplies, little things like that."

"What does that have to do with the attempts on Nicole's life?" Yes, I'd already come to the conclusion independently that someone was indeed trying to kill Grace's boss. One accident is possible, but two, so close together? No, I wasn't buying it, especially with the dismantled detector as additional evidence.

"Nothing that I know of. I just thought it was interesting."

"What about Georgia?"

"She's a real piece of work," Grace said as she suddenly yanked the steering wheel to the right, nearly sending us off the road into the woods far below. I hadn't been paying too much attention to the drop-off on my side before then, but seeing it up close had made me stomp on imaginary brakes on my side of the car. "Sorry," she apologized as she corrected her steering back to the road. "I thought I saw a groundhog."

"I didn't see anything," I said.

"It was there, Suzanne. Maybe that's why they call this area the Shadow Mountains. It's really hard to see the road clearly with all of these trees looming over it."

It was time to get back on point. We were running out of time, and I could feel my ears popping from the change in air pressure. It was getting a bit chillier as well, and I started to wonder if I'd packed enough heavy clothes to get me through the long weekend. "Tell me about Georgia."

"She'd climb over your dead body if she wanted what was on the other side, no questions asked, and no looking back. I could see her trying to run Nicole over without a problem, but I'm not sure she's devious enough to think of the pilot light."

"So then, we have two obvious suspects. That should make it easier than most of our cases have been in the past."

Grace shook her head. "Sorry, but there's more."

"Why wouldn't there be? Who else belongs on the list?"

"There are two other people in Nicole's life who might want to see her dead as well: her sister, Celia, and her intermittent fiancé, Hank Lancaster. Oh, I forgot to mention something. Hank is the district manager who arranged that little competition for the job Nicole now has."

This was getting messier by the second.

I sighed heavily, and Grace didn't miss it. "I know. It's a real mess, isn't it?"

"Let's take these one at a time. Why would her own sister want her dead?"

"When Nicole's parents died, they left Nicole in charge of everything, and I mean completely. Celia had a long history of burning through her money at an alarming rate, and now Nicole metes it out in small sums, and Celia isn't shy about letting everyone know that she resents it."

"And if something happens to Nicole?"

"Then Celia gets everything the moment she's pronounced dead," Grace said.

"Wow, it sounds as though she has reason enough if the estate is of any size at all."

"From what I've heard, it's well over a million dollars," she told me.

"Okay, that's a motive. How about Hank? Why would he want to kill her?"

"After Nicole got the promotion, she broke up with him, once and for all. She knows that he can't fire her because of it, and she's gotten it on the company record, just in case he tries. She's bulletproof from one kind of termination, but not the more final one."

Wow. Just wow. I would not want to be in this woman's shoes for love or money. "Okay, it appears that we've got our work cut out for us."

"I'm sorry I got you into this jam. The good news is that all of our suspects will be gathered together for the entire three-day weekend."

"Even Celia?"

"She's Nicole's plus one," Grace said. "We thought it would be easier that way."

"It's hard enough as it is," I said as I pointed out a massive towering oak tree over the road that looked as though it had been there forever. The tree was so large that, for a single moment, it completely blocked out the sun as we drove under it.

"Sorry I got you into this," Grace said. "It's not too late to back out, you know."

"I'm afraid that it is," I said as I pointed out the sign that stood tall as we broke through the last of the trees that crowded the road on both sides.

The sign read, "*Welcome to Shadow Mountain Resort, Your Final Destination.*"

I didn't like the sound of that at all.

CHAPTER 4

THE RESORT WAS BREATHTAKING; THERE was no doubt about that. The main lodge had been built on a hilltop, grand in a way that wouldn't be possible to replicate today, with heavy woods situated just behind and on the right side of it. The walls were made from heavy fieldstone, and small windows were scattered along its front. Three massive chimneys stood high in the sky above the tile rooflines, and smoke wafted gently from two of them at the moment. Off to the left, built on a much smaller scale, were four cottages, each constructed from identical matching stone, and every one of them situated on the edge of what appeared to be a steep drop-off to the forest below. These cottages were accessible from a gravel footpath alone. In the other direction was a large lake, pristine in its surroundings, with nothing but a boat house, a fire pit with benches, and a gazebo spaced out along its edges. Finally, where a grand lawn most likely should have been, there was a dense copse of evergreens, and I saw a faded sign that proclaimed it to be a maze. That should be interesting. I'd had a bad experience the last time I'd been in one, but it had been made of corn stalks, not living trees.

As we parked on the right side of the building and got out of Grace's car, I could see that several other parties had already arrived. Pulling my light jacket closer, I had an involuntary shudder from the chill. "It's really cold up here, isn't it?" Grace asked me with a grin. "I'm not sure I packed enough warm clothes to get me through three days."

"I'm not sure I'll have enough to get me through today," I said. "Where do we go now?"

"We're supposed to go to the main lodge front entrance," Grace said as we puzzled out the front of the building. Long and low rooflines were just off the first level, giving the place the feeling of a single long eyebrow, and it wasn't until we walked up the stone steps that I realized that it was one massive porch, under cover from rain, and probably snow as well, given the temperatures we were experiencing at the moment. There was a scattering of tables and chairs spread out along the terrace, and I could see the entrance at last, a grand old wooden door that looked as though it hadn't been touched since it had been put in place a century before.

Once we were inside the building, the place was even more magnificent. Stone walls and floors gave the grand space an open feeling, and heart-pine wood covered the sweeping vaulted ceiling. An iron chandelier hung in the center of the room, and the far wall was taken up by a massive fireplace. There were comfortable couches and chairs surrounding it, and the registration desk was opposite it, ready to welcome the resort's guests. Beside the desk were steps leading upstairs, and on the right side of the building, there was a sign indicating that the restaurant and bar were close by.

We approached the front desk, and Grace identified herself. "We're here with Laurel Cosmetics," she said.

The young man at the front desk gave us a clearly well-rehearsed smile. "Welcome to Shadow Mountain Lodge. Most of your party has already checked in." He slid a packet across the oak desktop toward her. "Everything you need is inside. I hope you enjoy your stay with us."

"Could we have our room keys?" Grace asked him. "We'd like to drop off our things first."

"They're in your packet," he said, tapping the thick envelope.

I was headed for the stairs when he stopped me. "Sorry, but you're not staying in the main lodge."

"What?" Grace asked. "Why not?"

"I was told that the top employees of your organization were awarded space in one of our cottages. You and your guest will be in the Hemlock Cottage."

I wasn't sure I liked that idea very much, for several reasons. Those cottages were secluded from the main lodge. We'd have to trudge back and forth for meals and other activities, and that included nighttime and any foul weather we might be getting while we were there. Also, hemlock was poisonous, wasn't it?

Clearly Grace didn't care for the idea very much, either.

"Is there any way we could switch and stay here in the lodge?" she asked.

"I'm afraid that would be impossible. You see, we're extended beyond the end of our season, and we're working with a short staff. Trust me, you'll love your cottage. They're the best we have to offer."

"Sweet, then Hemlock it is," I said, trying my best to make Grace think it was a wonderful idea. "Let's go check it out."

"Grace? Hello. Glad you made it. We're all in here," a lovely woman in her mid-thirties called out to us from the restaurant. Though we both had dark hair, mine was simply brown, while hers could best be described as chestnut, full of rich tones of deep browns and reds. Her green eyes were set off by porcelain skin, and if that's what their line of makeup did, I was beginning to think I'd been too rash turning Grace's offers of free cosmetics down in the past.

Grace said softly, "That's Nicole."

"Hi," Grace told her boss as we approached. "Sorry we're

late." I could see what she meant about her new boss's expensive tastes. Nicole was dressed pretty elegantly, from her shoes to her dress to her jewelry, and I knew that Gabby Williams, a woman in April Springs who sold gently used designer clothing in a shop called ReNEWed, would have loved to get her hands on anything Nicole was wearing.

The restaurant sported half a dozen large tables, while the front contained a modest bar with a walk-through to the patio. I could see another pair of outdoor tables and chairs there.

Grace said, "Nicole, this is Suzanne Hart. Suzanne, I'd like you to meet my boss, Nicole Thurman."

"It's a pleasure to meet you," she said, enfolding my hand in both of hers. "I've heard so much about you."

"Thanks," I said, not quite sure how to respond to that.

In a low voice, she said, "I really appreciate you helping me out. We'll talk later, okay?"

"Sounds good," I replied as other women began to join us. Grace made the introductions in rapid-fire order. I had to admit, they were a nice-looking group of women, and I felt positively dowdy being among them. I took special note when she introduced Janelle Best and Georgia Collier. Georgia looked a little like a fox, with long, thin features and small eyes, while Janelle was fuller in both face and figure. Neither one of them looked like a potential murderer, but then again, it had been my experience in the past that I could never tell what a killer was supposed to look like.

"Oh, and this is my sister, Celia," Nicole said. As I shook her hand, I couldn't help but compare her unfavorably to Nicole. Celia was washed out somehow, a faded image of her sister's beauty, just a shade short of pretty. She carried more weight than any of the other women there, including me, and her hair was a shade of dirty blonde that lacked any kind of luster at all. Suddenly I didn't feel quite so plain anymore.

"Where's Hank?" Grace asked Nicole.

"Late, as usual," she replied when we heard a commotion in the lobby. A man was speaking at the top of his voice, and most of the women looked hesitantly toward the restaurant door. "It appears that he made it after all."

A tall, heavyset man with thick brown hair joined us, a frown on his face. "What's this nonsense about putting me in a cottage, Nicole?" he asked her as he walked toward us.

"They're the nicest accommodations in the resort," she said, "but if you'd like to be moved to the main lodge, I'm sure that last-minute arrangements can be made. I should warn you that the rooms here are substantially smaller, though, and with no real housekeeping, you'll have to take care of cleaning yourself."

"No, that's fine. I'll stay out in the boondocks, if that's the way you set things up. You're out there as well, I suppose?"

Nicole nodded. "You've got one cottage, my sister and I have another, Grace and Suzanne have one, and Georgia and Janelle are sharing the last one. Given the short staff here at the resort, they felt that we'd all be happier with our own cottages."

Hank looked at Georgia and Janelle and grinned, though there was no humor in it at all. "Doubling up, are you?"

"Nicole asked us if we wouldn't mind, given the short staffing issues," Janelle said. "We were happy to do it."

"It's fine," Georgia added.

"Surprise!" a woman announced as she burst into the dining room.

She hurried toward Nicole, who frowned for just a moment. "Dina, what are you doing here?"

"I thought I'd take a chance on getting a room and driving up on my own," the bottle blonde said. "You made it sound so lovely that I couldn't resist. Surely there's room for me here as well." She looked around before adding, "This place is massive."

"I'm not sure that they can accommodate you," Nicole said,

and then she introduced the woman to us en masse. "This is Dina Harmon, everyone."

"Hello one and all," Dina said. She had a big personality, and it was pretty clear that Nicole not only hadn't been expecting her, but she wasn't all that pleased by her presence.

"Well, now that we're all here, let's get down to business, shall we?" Hank asked. Then he turned to me, Celia, and Dina. Evidently the others had ignored the plus-one part of the invitation. "If you ladies will excuse us, we have some business to attend to before we begin the other activities."

Nicole frowned again. "Activities? I hadn't planned anything for us as a group."

"No worries on that front. I've already handled it," Hank said, giving her a sharp-eyed look that dared her to defy him. He might not be able to fire her because of their recent relationship, but clearly he wasn't above throwing his weight around as her direct supervisor.

Nicole shrugged, and Grace looked at me apologetically. "Here, Suzanne. Take the packet. It's got our keys in it."

"Sorry, but you'll be needing that as well," Hank said.

Grace looked at him and smiled, but I knew it lacked any hint of sincerity. As she dug out my key, she whispered, "Sorry about this."

"No worries," I said as I took it and, along with Celia and Dina, left them to it.

I decided to linger in the main quarters before I went off in search of the Hemlock cottage. I found a bulletin board behind glass that displayed photographs there from the 1920s and '30s, along with menus, activity sheets, and registers from past seasons offering up the names of movie stars, titans of industry and politics, and even a few authors. There was a bookshelf near the fireplace that offered titles across the decades, and I browsed through a few before returning them to their places. There was a fire gently burning away in the hearth, and I was watching the flames when someone nearby spoke to me. "You're Grace's friend, right?"

Celia Thurman was studying me as though I were some kind of oddity. "That's right, I am."

"Are you two *together*?" she asked me. What kind of question was that? Then I realized that she was asking me if we were a couple.

"No, we've been best friends since we were kids. I'm married to the chief of police, and Grace is dating his lieutenant." Celia didn't seem all that interested in me after that, and I had to wonder if I'd already begun to bore her with my mundane life.

"How nice for both of you," she said.

"Your sister seems really nice," I said, watching her closely for some kind of reaction. "You're lucky to have her."

Celia was about to say something sharp when she stopped herself. "Lucky. That describes me to a tee. Yes, I don't know what I'd do without Nicole watching out for me." There was definitely a hint of anger in her voice, no matter how she might try to disguise it.

"I think Nicole is fabulous," Dina said as she joined us.

"You two aren't even friends anymore, Dina, and you know it. What are you doing here?" Celia asked her.

"What? That's nonsense. What makes you say that?"

"You can drop the act. Nicole trusted you with her savings, and you lost most of it before she fired you as her financial advisor."

"The market had a correction. There was nothing I could do about it," Dina said, a slight crack appearing in her armor. "Besides, that was business. This is personal. Just because we had a slight hiccup in her account doesn't mean that we stopped being good friends."

"Maybe according to you, but that's not the way Nicole tells it."

"I'm sure you're mistaken, Celia," Dina said, trying her best to smile.

"You make me weary," Celia said as she stood and left us without another word, heading for the bar.

"You're not supposed to go in there," Dina called out.

Celia just waved a hand in the air and continued anyway.

After a moment, Dina said, "She was always difficult, even as a child."

"Have you known them that long?" I asked her.

"Oh, we've been friends forever. That's why this little misunderstanding has troubled me so. I need the opportunity to make Nicole see that none of this was my fault, so I figured, what better way to talk her out of pursuing any legal action than to face her directly?"

"She's suing you?" I asked.

"Nicole said it in the heat of the moment, but I'm sure that I'll be able to smooth things over with her once I get the opportunity. So, what do you do for a living, Suzanne?"

"I make donuts," I said.

She patted my shoulder gently. "Don't worry. I'm sure something better will come along for you soon. Chin up, and all that."

"I happen to own the business, and I'm perfectly happy with how I make my living."

"I'm sure you are," she said condescendingly. "I might see if Celia was able to get that drink after all. I'm a bit parched myself."

After she was gone, I felt sorry for Nicole. Her boss was a jerk, her sister a weight on her back, and her so-called friend had lost a good deal of her money. Not only that, but two of the women she'd beaten out for her job clearly resented her very presence. At least she had Grace on her side. I was more determined than ever to do what I could to figure out exactly what was going on.

In the meantime, it was as good a time as any to check out the Hemlock cottage and see what it was like.

At least that's the direction I started off in.

CHAPTER 5

M AZES HAVE INTRIGUED ME SINCE I was a little girl. A farmer outside April Springs used to do a corn maze long before they became popular, and Grace and I had dragged my mother along every chance we got. After awhile, Momma grew tired and frustrated, and she'd tap one of the guides to lead her out, costing her a dollar that she always gladly paid. That was pure genius on the farmer's part, in my mind. Not only did he charge admission, but most folks ended up paying to get out, too. Over the years, Grace and I had become rather adept at finding our way out, something that had helped me in our investigations, allowing me to escape from a killer once. I shivered a little at the memory, realizing once again how close I'd come to becoming his next victim. This was different, in many ways. While that maze, much like the ones from my childhood, had been impermanent by its very nature, this one was made from some kind of evergreen, dark and rich and lush, created to stand the test of time. As I neared the entrance, I saw that the sign announcing the maze had a hinged top, and glancing underneath it, I realized that the owners had outlined the way to beat the maze in a record amount of time. I dropped the top back down as though it had burned me. That was cheating, and if Grace and I tackled it later, I wanted to beat the maze honestly. Otherwise what was the point? It was like someone who read the last few pages of a mystery novel to see if they liked the outcome and only then decided to read the book from the beginning. If I lived forever, I would never understand that type of person. Live and let live, though. I knew that many people found my occupational choice more than slightly south of sane, but I wouldn't trade my little donut shop for the world.

I decided to leave the maze for later and walked over to the edge of the lake. Perhaps calling it a lake was a little too generous. Just how big did a body of water have to be to go from a pond to a lake? I decided to check it on my cellphone, as I'd recently learned how to do Internet searches on it, but alas, there was no service up on the mountaintop. Zero bars. That meant that I wouldn't be talking to my husband, either, but then again, Jake would probably be too busy to chat anyway. I smiled a little as I put my phone away, imagining how Type-A-personality Hank would react to being completely out of touch with the rest of the world.

In the end, I decided to call it a lake, since that's what the brochure had named it. There were two structures near the water, a boathouse that I found was closed for the season upon closer examination and a gazebo that offered benches overlooking the water. I sat on one for a few minutes, and I was rewarded by seeing five ducks fly in and settle on its still surface. I could have stayed out there longer, but I was a bit chilly, so I decided to go over to Hemlock and see what it was like.

As I walked toward the gravel path, I noticed that the land behind the cottages seemed to drop off the face of the earth, as though it was some kind of ending point for land. Skirting the gravel path, I took two steps toward the drop and found a forest far below me, dense woods growing at such a steep angle that I knew one misstep could be my last. There wasn't even a guardrail there, not even a slim chain to warn walkers of imminent death below. How many guests had they lost over the years to its descent? Then I noticed intermittent holes in the ground along the path, and I realized that they must be replacing whatever had stood guard there before. It would be prudent to be careful walking along that gravel in the interim, though, especially at night.

I was a little alarmed to see the door to our cottage standing slightly ajar. Pushing it open, I called out, "Grace? Are you there?"

But it was empty.

Perhaps someone in housekeeping had failed to latch it securely after they'd left. I shrugged it off to someone being in a hurry, and I looked around. The cabin was cozy, but it lacked the grandeur of the lodge, though the buildings had been constructed out of similar materials. For one thing, the windows seemed tiny in comparison, and they failed to let in much natural light. Two twin beds, a nightstand, and a dresser occupied one wall, while a desk and chair were along the other. I peeked into the small bathroom and found small white-and-black tiles covering the floor. It had the standard facilities there, even though the shower was rather small compared to my modern tastes. I was sure that it would be fine, and I wondered what had happened to Grace. Were they still meeting inside? I'd been meandering around for quite some time, and I'd half-expected to find her in the cottage by the time I got there, but there was no sign that she'd even been there.

Being careful to latch the door and lock it behind me, I set off for Grace's car to get our bags. When I got there, though, I was thwarted.

It was locked, and Grace had the keys.

I decided I couldn't face running into Celia or Dina again, so I grabbed one of the chairs on the terrace or patio or veranda or whatever they called it and looked out onto the mountains below us. A mist was starting to climb up the valley floor, looking like spun sugar, and a breeze began to blow. It was time to go inside until I could get some warmer clothes on. If I ran into anyone else, I'd do my best to get along with them, but I was beginning to wonder if I'd done the right thing coming along with Grace on this trip.

To my surprise, I nearly ran into my best friend as I walked in. "There you are," she said. "I've been looking all over for you."

"I decided to take the grand walking tour while you were tied up," I said. I noticed that she had a pair of hooded sweatshirts in her hands. "What are those for?"

"They're part of this team-building exercise," she said as she threw one to me.

"Does this mean that I'm on the team, too?" I asked with a grin as I pulled it on over my light shirt and thin jacket. The warmth was most welcome.

"Don't feel too special. Everybody gets one," Grace said.

"Even Dina?"

"That was odd, wasn't it? I have no idea what that was all about."

"I can help you out there," I said. After I brought Grace up to speed on what I'd learned so far from Celia and Dina, she smiled at me. "What's so amusing?"

"You can't help yourself from detecting, can you?" she asked. "It looks as though we've just added another suspect to our list."

"As if we needed another one," I said softly. "I'm beginning to feel sorry for Nicole."

"I know, right?" Grace asked. "She deserves better than this."

"Hopefully we'll be able to tell her who she needs to watch out for by the time this three-day weekend is over," I said.

"I've got faith in us. Are you hungry?"

"You know me," I replied with a grin. "I can always eat."

"Good, because Hank has decided that we'll all be living by his schedule while we're here."

"What exactly does that mean?"

"In bed by nine, and up by six," she said with a groan. "Some retreat this is turning out to be."

"Look on the bright side," I said.

"What's that?"

"For me, it will be staying up late and sleeping in," I answered, reminding her of my brutal hours running Donut Hearts.

"At least somebody will be happy. So what do you say? Are you ready?"

"I can't wait," I said as I followed Grace back into the dining room.

The staff had set the tables in my absence, and I was surprised to find a nametag at every chair. "If I'm not sitting with you, I'm going home," I told her.

"Don't worry. We're together," she replied and led us to our seats.

I glanced around to see who would be joining us.

I saw Nicole's name and her sister's at our table. I wondered if she'd arranged things that way, and I decided that, given the group, it was probably the best result I could hope for, as long as I didn't have to make any more small talk with Celia.

I looked around, but there wasn't a waiter in sight. I didn't even have water in my glass. I was about to say something when Hank stood. There was a wicked grin on his face, and I wondered what he was up to.

I didn't have long to find out.

"As you all know, I believe that how we play games is a good indication of how we handle life, and this weekend is no exception. I'm sure most of you have noticed the absence of waitstaff. Don't blame the resort. They're acting on my instructions. This evening, you're all going to have to sing for your supper."

"But I can't sing," Janelle Best complained.

"Not literally," Hank said, looking at her with open contempt. "I'm talking about solving riddles and puzzles before

33

you've earned the right to eat. The prize is worth it. I've had the chef prepare a sumptuous meal. I just hope that at least some of you have the opportunity to enjoy it."

There were a few murmured protests, but after everyone had seen the way he'd handled Janelle, no one was willing to say anything out loud. "Don't worry, even if you fail tonight, you won't go hungry. You see, there's a time limit on the challenge. Anyone not back here by nine o'clock will get a cheese sandwich and a bottle of water. That's fair, isn't it?"

"What's the first puzzle?" Georgia asked, obviously intent on being finished first.

"It's in the display case in the front hall. Oh, there's one more thing. Cheating won't be tolerated." Was he looking at Georgia and Janelle as he said that? "You must visit every solution yourself, and if you don't, I'll know it."

We all looked at each other, and a few folks started to stand when Hank added, "Sit back down. This is a team challenge as well. I want to see how well you work with others. Dina, since you weren't invited to this event, you won't be participating."

"Does that mean that I don't get to eat?" she asked him petulantly.

Hank considered the question, and then he smiled as he said, "If all of the other teams solve the riddles, then you will dine with us. Otherwise, you'll have to eat with the losers. If you are unhappy with that proposal, you're free to leave at any time."

"No, that sounds fine to me," she said, though it was clear that it was anything but.

Hank nodded, and then he pulled out a large hat as he explained, "I've entered each of your names into the drawing, so the pairings will be fair."

I looked at Grace, who shrugged apologetically. I frowned in return, but I didn't hold it very long. After all, this silly contest hadn't been her idea, so I could hardly blame her for it.

"Suzanne Hart," Hank called out from the front. "Stand up, please."

I did as instructed, though for a moment, I thought about refusing his order. I wasn't in the mood to play his game, but I was there representing Grace, so I couldn't let her down. I stood up, and he drew the next name. "Nicole Thurman," he announced.

At least I'd been paired with someone I liked. I would have chosen Grace if I'd been given the option, but this might not be too bad.

We smiled at each other, and Hank said, "Well, what are you waiting for? Go."

"That's not fair," Georgia said. "They get a head start."

"This game, much like life, never claimed to be fair," Hank replied.

I nodded to Grace as Nicole and I left.

"Good luck," she said.

"Right back at you."

"Sorry about this," Nicole said as we walked out into the lobby. "I'm afraid that Hank thinks he's clever. He's writing a motivational book, if you can believe that. I don't know what I ever saw in him in the first place."

"Well, he's certainly good looking, in a rugged kind of way," I said.

Nicole frowned. "I know. That's what trapped me in the first place. Unfortunately, that pretty wrapping conceals a fairly obnoxious gift inside."

"It's interesting to find a man working in the cosmetics industry, isn't it?" I asked her.

"His mother was one of the company's founders, so she found a place for her son when he couldn't hold a job doing anything else. Never mind Hank, though. Why don't we try to make this fun in spite of him?"

"That sounds good to me," I said as I headed for the bulletin board I'd studied earlier.

There was a new addition to it.

The world is full of amazing things,
Puzzles are everywhere.
Who knows just what our fortune brings,
When we try hard enough to dare?

"Wow, that's a really weak poem," Nicole said with the hint of a smile. "Hank fancies himself a wordsmith, and he used to write me poetry that was every bit as bad as this. What is this even supposed to mean?"

"Unless I'm mistaken, it's got the answer in the very first line," I said as I headed for the front door. "I can't believe that he actually used the word 'maze' in his clue."

"Honestly, that's kind of clever," Nicole said as she joined me. "Do we have to solve the maze out front? I've never been good at that sort of thing."

"Don't worry, I'm a seasoned pro at it."

When we got to the maze's entrance, I was ready to start inside right away when Nicole asked, "What's under here?" as she lifted the lid I'd checked out earlier.

She was right, of course. Why try to solve the maze ourselves when the solution had already been presented to us? She lifted the lid, and I moved in to study the solution.

It read, "*Two lefts, two rights, one left, one right,*" and it showed a diagram as well.

We both went in together, and with the map in my head, we quickly found the center.

Surprise, surprise. The next clue was there indeed, along

with three duplicates of the cheap childhood plastic game where little steel balls had to be led through a maze by moving the entire game from side to side. I'd had one as a child, but I'd grown bored with it after quickly mastering its secrets. The sign said, *"Take One,"* so I did, and we moved on to the next clue.

"Water, water, everywhere,
And tasks before you're fed,
Look around but try not to stare,
At the angles above your head."

"Did he mean to write 'angels'"? Nicole asked me.

"I don't think so," I said as I puzzled it out aloud. "Water implies proximity to the lake, and angles means that it must be in a structure nearby."

"Does that mean that we should go to the boathouse?" Nicole suggested.

"No, unless I miss my guess, it's got to be the gazebo," I said, heading out of the maze in reverse order of the way that we'd come in. "The clue about angles gives it away. The boathouse is locked, but I can still see that it's a rectangle, while the gazebo is an octagon, full of all kinds of odd angles."

"How did you know that?" Nicole asked me as we broke out of the maze. Grace was just coming out of the lodge, with Georgia in the lead. She looked unhappy about the pairing, and who could blame her? There was nothing I could do about it, though, so I waved to her as we rushed forward.

The floor and benches of the gazebo were devoid of any further clues, but between two rafters, there was a new clue, as well as three little octagons made of wood and painted green. Nicole grabbed a piece as I read the puzzle.

This next clue is hidden among the trees,

Though they've never been alive,
You'll have to get down on your hands and knees,
Or of dinner you will be deprived.

"Clumsy rhythm to the rhyme," Nicole said, puzzled. "But what does it mean?"

I thought about it for a few moments, and then I realized that the cottage names were all trees, and the stones forming them had never been alive. "Let's go."

"Where?" Nicole asked.

"To the cottages," I said as I raced toward them.

"But what's the clue mean?"

"It has to be the names of the cottages themselves: Pine, Spruce, Fir, Hemlock."

"I'm beginning to think I lucked out in the partner drawing," Nicole said.

"I've always been fond of puzzles," I said.

The only problem was that we couldn't find the next clue when we got there.

CHAPTER 6

I WAS ABOUT TO GIVE UP when Nicole said, "Suzanne! Over here! I found it!"

I joined her in the narrow space between Pine and Spruce and found her literally down on her knees. "It was under this big rock," she said.

I looked at the hiding place and realized that this particular stone didn't match any of the others I'd seen at the resort. When I lifted it, it came up with surprising ease.

Nicole grinned at me. "That fooled me, too. It's made from Styrofoam."

"Nice spot," I said.

Underneath the rock, there was another puzzle and three small river stones, smoothed from ages of being exposed to running water. Nicole grabbed a stone in triumph as I read the next clue.

Some fires burn bright
But some are for show
This one is light
But cannot glow

I stared at it a few seconds, and then I turned to Nicole. "Sorry, but I'm stumped by this one. I don't have a clue."

"Neither do I," she admitted.

Out loud, I asked, "How can a fire be for show only here? The only fireplaces I saw in the main lodge were real ones."

"Let's think about it. What can be a fire for show?" she asked me.

"My aunt had a heater that displayed fake flames," I said, "but something like that seems out of place here."

"What choice do we have? It's the only idea we've been able to come up with, so it's worth a shot, but where do we start?"

I thought about it for a moment before I spoke. "It would have to be in a public space, wouldn't it? How about the lodge? Have you seen anything like he's describing?"

"No, but that doesn't mean that it's not there. Let's go check," she said.

"I'm not at all certain that we're even getting warm with this guess," I replied as we headed back to where we'd started this silly game.

"It's more than I've been able to come up with, so we might as well try," she said.

We went inside the main lodge to find Hank waiting for us. He wasn't smiling, though he should have been. After all, he was controlling this little party, and I was fairly certain that he wouldn't miss tonight's meal, even if he had to eat alone. "How are you two doing so well? This was supposed to be harder than you're making it seem."

Nicole smiled at him. "That's because Suzanne's good with puzzles."

"Don't sell yourself short, Nicole. You've been helping, too," I said.

"Well, the next clue's the toughest of all," Hank said with wicked delight.

"Is it fair, though? That's the real question," I asked him.

Hank scowled at me, his attractiveness dissipating like fresh rain on a hot pavement. "Are you accusing me of something, Suzanne?"

Nicole stepped between us. "She just wants to know if this puzzle is solvable."

He shrugged slightly. "It's not easy, if that's what you're asking, but if you're smart enough, you'll be able to figure it out."

I wanted nothing more at that moment than to wipe that smug look off his face. He could keep his gourmet meal; I just wanted to win now. "Come on, Nicole. Let's get busy with our search."

Hank was still frowning at me, but I couldn't care less if I tried. Where could the next clue be hiding? I looked around the fireplace, which was blazing now, but there was nothing there. I happened to glimpse Hank, and I saw that he was smiling broadly. It just made me more determined than ever to figure this out. There were no other fires in the reception area, though.

Nicole came over and asked me softly, "Suzanne, are we sure about this?"

"No. I mean yes," I quickly amended.

"Why the sudden change of heart?"

"Would Hank have been waiting for us if the next clue hadn't been here?" I asked. "Or would he have been out on the front porch where he could watch us all scurrying around like mice? It's somewhere nearby. I can feel it in my bones."

"Then let's keep looking."

Nicole started leafing through the magazines and books, while I studied the room as a whole. I'd noticed the photographs and paintings on my earlier visit. Could a clue be hidden among them? It all suddenly made sense. The fire could be printed or painted, giving off the appearance of light but without heat! And both were meant for show, just as the clue warned.

I approached Nicole and told her my theory quietly so Hank couldn't overhear me.

"It's got to be it," she said. "You take that side, and I'll start over here."

As we moved along the walls and started studying the

paintings and photographs, I looked over at Hank again and saw that his frown had returned. We were onto something!

Two minutes later, Nicole called out, "Here it is! I found it!"

I joined her at a large framed photograph I'd somehow missed before. It had been treated with something to make it appear old, but there was something about it that made me realize that it wasn't original to the lodge. The scene was one of nighttime, and a familiar-looking fire pit blazed in its center. That was it. No words, no cheesy poetry, just the fire pit. I was about to tell Nicole it was a red herring when I spotted three wooden matches lined up on the bottom edge of the frame.

"These must be the tokens," I said as I grabbed one.

"But where's the clue?" she asked.

I thought about it, and then I realized what it had to mean. "I've got a hunch that this one's literal. There's a fire pit out by the lake. The next clue's got to be there."

Hank had tried to listen to our whispered conversation, but he hadn't had any luck from the signs of frustration on his face. "Play along with me. This might be fun," I said softly to her, and then, in a much louder voice for Hank's benefit, I added, "I don't know, Nicole. Maybe he's stumped us with this one after all."

"Let's go back to the last clue and see if we missed something," she said and then winked at me.

Hank looked absolutely triumphant when we left the lodge.

Instead of wandering around, though, we headed straight to the fire pit by the lake.

There, inside the empty pit, were three bottle rockets and a short note.

"Congratulations! You've won!
Make it back to the dining room in time,
Get yourself ready for some fun,

Then you'll have a chance to fine dine!"

"That's the worst one yet," Nicole said. "Do we take this back with us, too?" she asked as she picked up one of the bottle rockets.

"No, I think we're supposed to shoot it off with the match we found in the lodge. That's how Hank will know if anyone is trying to cheat. Would you like to do the honors?" I asked her as I handed her the match.

"No, we couldn't have done it without you," Nicole said. "You go ahead."

I placed our rocket in one of the three empty soda bottles lined up outside the pit and lit the fuse. Taking a step back to rejoin Nicole, we watched as it shot upward and arched over the lake, exploding at the end of its flight and sending sparks cascading down to the water.

"What do we take back, the burnt match or the bottle? There's no way we can retrieve that rocket from where it landed."

"Let's take them both," I said. I noticed the other teams watching us. Grace was the only one smiling.

We made it back to the front porch, where Hank was waiting on us. "I have to admit, that was clever," he said. "Do you have the talismans?" He wanted to deny us our victory; I could see it in his gaze.

I laid them out, one at a time: the game, the octagon, the burnt match, and the bottle.

"Sorry. That's not right," he said smugly.

"What? It has to be," Nicole protested. "We did everything by the book. If you didn't want us to fire off that rocket, why give us matches in the first place? You said you'd play fair, Hank!"

"I have," he said smugly, glancing down at our tokens again.

That's when I got it. I reached for the puzzle and saw him scowling again. In thirty seconds, I had every ball in its proper place and put the game back down carefully so I wouldn't dislodge any of them.

"How about now?" I asked.

He nodded, his lips making two grim little lines.

"So, when do we eat?" I asked him happily. I didn't care if I made him mad or not. After all, he wasn't *my* boss.

"When it's time," Hank said stiffly. "Now, if you'll excuse me, the others are still working on their puzzles." He was nearly at the door when he said, "I meant what I said about not cheating. You are not to give hints, clues, gestures, glances, or any other form of assistance to any of the others, or you will be disqualified. Is that understood?"

Nicole nodded, but I chose to salute instead.

After Hank was gone, she giggled like a teenager. "He didn't like that one bit, did he?"

"That's just too bad," I said. "Let's go see how the others are doing. We might not be able to help them, but we can at least be there to lend moral support."

CHAPTER 7

I T WAS CLOSE, BUT A few minutes before the deadline was upon us, the last pairing of Janelle and Celia made it in, carrying their tokens with them. I noted that Janelle had solved the puzzle on the walk in, and when they were in place, matching ours, Hank put on a false smile. "Very well. Everyone accomplished their tasks. Let's eat, shall we?"

We all followed him into the dining room, where a sumptuous meal was waiting for us. We dined on crab puffs, shrimp cocktail, roast pork, salmon, glazed asparagus, garlic mashed potatoes, steamed vegetables, and for dessert, there was a choice between chocolate mousse or fresh berries and cream. I would never have admitted it to Hank, but it had been a meal worth every moment we'd spent working for it.

After the meal was finished, I found myself yawning, and not just because of the feast. It was nearing my bedtime, and I was having a hard time staying awake.

I approached Grace and Nicole, who were deep in conversation about something business related. "If you all don't mind, I think I'm going to call it a night."

"Okay," Grace said as she stood. "I'll go with you."

"Nonsense. You don't have to babysit me. You two keep talking. I'll be fine."

"Don't forget to pick up a flashlight on your way out,"

Nicole said. "That treasure hunt was fun, Suzanne. I'm glad we were partners."

"So am I," I said.

"Suzanne, are you sure you don't mind if I hang back for awhile?" Grace asked.

"Honestly, it's fine. I don't mind at all," I said.

I was retrieving one of the flashlights when I heard Nicole call out from behind me, "Hang on a second, Suzanne. I'll keep you company."

"You're not going to bed, too, are you?"

"No, but I need to get my laptop, and I already dropped it off at my cottage. There's something I want to show Grace."

"Okay then, let's go."

We walked out together into the night air, and I realized that it had gotten much cooler out while we'd been inside dining by the warm fireplace in the restaurant. I was glad that we'd all been issued hooded sweatshirts for the weekend, but heavy parkas might have been even better. I zipped my sweatshirt closed and jammed my hands in the pockets as we stepped out onto the porch and turned our flashlights on.

"It's freezing, isn't it?" Nicole asked as we hurried our pace.

"I'm glad you all provided these sweatshirts," I said. "I'm still going to have to wear more layers than I'd planned on."

Our feet crunched on the gravel, and I played my light over the maze for a moment. "Hank thought he was being sneaky using that, didn't he?"

"I'm not entirely positive that he knew the solution was under the sign," she answered with a giggle. "No wonder he was so upset when we cracked his puzzles so quickly."

"How has he been treating you since you broke up with him?" I asked her gently.

Nicole hesitated a moment, and then she said, "Better than I expected him to, as a matter of fact. Before you and Grace got here, Hank pulled me aside, and I thought I was in for another argument with him, but he told me that he understood and that it was okay."

"As though you needed his permission to break up with him in the first place," I said.

"No, it wasn't like that at all. I think we're going to be fine, as a matter of fact. I don't think you and Grace need to even consider him as one of our candidates for what's been happening to me."

"Maybe it's just a clever cover," I said as we neared the four cottages.

"From Hank? He's really not all that shrewd," she said. Hemlock was the cottage closest to the main lodge and where Grace and I were staying. We got there first, but instead of stopping, I asked, "Do you mind if I walk you to your door?"

"Suzanne, you said it yourself. It's freezing out here. Go on. I'll be fine."

I considered doing exactly what she'd asked, but then I knew that if I did that, and something happened to her that I might have been able to prevent, I would never be able to forgive myself. "I don't mind. After that meal, I could use the exercise."

"Okay, if you're sure," she said, the relief heavy in her voice.

We walked past the two cottages with their signs naming them, Fir and Spruce, and then we were at Pine, the one Nicole was sharing with Celia and also farthest from the main lodge.

The other cottages had porch lights blazing like beacons, but Pine's was unlit.

"That's odd," I said. "I wonder why yours is off?"

"Maybe it's burned out or something," Nicole said.

"Hang on a second." I looked around for something to use as a weapon, just in case, and found a piece of narrow firewood near Spruce's front porch.

"What are you going to do with that?" Nicole asked me.

"I'm going to defend us from the bad guys, if there are any," I said.

As we approached the unlit porch, I firmed my grip on the thin log.

Nicole was about to go inside when I noticed from her light that her door was unlocked and standing slightly ajar as well. I pulled her back before she could go through. "Did you leave that door open the last time you left?" I asked her softly.

"No, I'm fairly certain that I locked it when I headed for the lodge, but Celia has a hard time remembering to lock things. It's probably nothing."

"That's what I thought when I found my door like that, but I still didn't take any chances. Stay behind me." Using the piece of firewood, I pushed the door open ahead of me, playing my light all around while still staying outside on the front porch.

There was a loud noise as something hit the floor hard at my feet! I'd seen something falling, and I'd instinctively jumped back, but if I'd walked through that door like nothing was wrong, whatever had fallen would have struck me squarely on top of the head. I played my flashlight beam on it and saw that it was another piece of firewood, one much more substantial than the one in my hands.

"What happened?" Nicole asked as she hurried in beside me.

"Someone rigged a little unwelcome surprise for you," I said.

Nicole started to walk in to get a better look at it, but I held her back. "Hang on. That might not be the only thing waiting inside for you." I slowly walked through the door, flipping on the light as I did. Barely glancing at the chunk of firewood, I did a quick inspection of the cottage, which didn't take very long, given that it was only two rooms, the main sleeping quarters and the bathroom. Everything looked to be fine, but I wasn't finished yet. I checked in the closet, under the beds, and even in the dresser drawers. I wasn't sure what I was expecting to find, but I knew that it was important to be thorough in my examination. It looked as though just the door's booby trap had been laid for her, as if that weren't enough. I hadn't realized I'd been holding my breath until I put the piece of wood in my hands down on the desk. While I'd been exploring the cottage, Nicole had hefted the wood that had been set as a trap for her and was studying it. "It looks just like the rest of the wood out there." Then she looked up at me, clearly appalled by what she'd just done. "I've just ruined the fingerprints, haven't I?"

I took the firewood from her and said, "I wouldn't worry about it if I were you. These surfaces are too rough to take prints, anyway. I'm guessing that whoever did this knew it and probably didn't even bother wearing gloves. It might not have hurt you badly, but you would have gotten a nasty headache if it had hit you on top of the head."

"Who would want to do that to me?" she asked, her voice on the verge of tears. "I just don't understand what's happening!"

"Nicole, it's clear that one of the folks we're looking at feels as though they have reason enough to harm you, even if it might not make sense to the rest of us."

"But Celia's eliminated as a suspect, isn't she?" she said, brightening a little. "Why would she set a trap that might just as easily have gotten her as me?"

"Sorry, but her name has to stay on our list," I said. "She was yawning well before I started, and yet she's still at the lodge. That makes me think that it's possible that she set this trap for you herself and then waited for you to fall for it. As far as I'm concerned, she has to still be a suspect."

"I don't know what to do," Nicole said.

"Watch your back at all times, and try not to take too many chances," I said.

"I wish I could stay with you and Grace tonight," she said.

"There's barely room for the two of us, but if you'd like, I'm sure we can work something out."

Nicole seemed to consider that, but then she shook her head. "Thanks, but I'll do what I'd planned to all along. I'd look like an idiot if I changed things at the last second."

"Don't be too hasty. The more I think about you staying with us, the more I believe that it might be the best thing that you could do," I said. "We might not get any real sleep tonight, but at least no one will be able to come after you without going through Grace and me first."

"Let me think about it," Nicole said.

"Fine, but I have a feeling that once Grace hears what just happened, she's not going to let it rest."

Nicole put her hands in mine for a moment. "Suzanne, do we really have to tell anybody else about what just happened?"

"Why should we keep it a secret?"

"I don't know. Maybe it will throw the killer off if we don't even react to it."

I supposed that it was possible, and honestly, what could it hurt? "Okay, on one condition. I get to tell Grace once I see her again."

"Does she really have to know?" Nicole asked.

"It's the only way I'll agree to the plan," I answered.

"Fine. But wait until she comes back to your room tonight. Would you at least do that for me?"

"I suppose I can concede that point." I picked up my flashlight, took the small piece of wood I'd chosen for a weapon, and then I said, "Grab your computer, and let's go back to the lodge."

"Are you coming back, too?"

"Just as far as the front door," I said. "I'm going to make sure you make it okay, and then I'm going back to Hemlock."

"You don't have to do that," Nicole said as she hesitated at the chunk of wood someone had tried to use against her, and then she finally picked it up.

"What are you going to do with that?" I asked her.

"I'm putting it out on the porch. The sight of it gives me the creeps." She did as she promised, and then we left the cottage together, being sure to lock the door behind us this time.

On a whim, when we approached Hemlock's front door, I tested the handle and was relieved to see that it was still locked. Nicole didn't comment on it, and we walked back to the lodge's front door together.

"Are you sure you don't want me to go inside with you?" I asked her.

"I'm positive. You mustn't worry about me. I'll be fine."

"Okay, but like I said before, don't take any chances. When Grace comes back to Hemlock, you go with her, no matter what else might happen. Will you promise me that much?"

"I promise. I have no desire to walk down that gravel path alone and in the dark," she said. "Thanks for looking out for me, Suzanne."

"My pleasure," I said.

After Nicole disappeared inside, I stood there debating whether I should rejoin them all despite how tired I was, but finally, I decided that it might not be the best idea. If I did something that counterintuitive, the killer might realize that I was in on Nicole's plan to keep the attempt to harm her quiet, and that might make me a target as well. It wasn't that I was afraid of getting a murderer's attention; goodness knows that I'd done that enough on my own in the past. It was that if I could keep my interest in the attempts to myself, then I might be able to catch the bad guy off guard unexpectedly.

I wasn't one hundred percent sure, though, and as I walked back along the graveled path, I couldn't help wondering if I was making the right decision after all.

CHAPTER 8

WHERE WAS GRACE, AND WHY hadn't she made it back to the cottage? I kept pacing around the tiny footprint of floor space, wondering why I hadn't just gone in when I'd walked Nicole back to the lodge. I'd hoped to get a little rest, but that was clearly not going to be happening. Finally, I put on the hooded sweatshirt I'd been issued, grabbed my flashlight, and headed back up the graveled path toward the main lodge alone.

And that was when I heard the first scream nearby, then the second, and finally, nothing at all.

CHAPTER 9

I NEARLY TRIPPED AS I RACED toward the lodge in the dark. "Grace? Nicole? Who just screamed? Are you okay?" The beam of my light was flying all around the resort's property, and it took nearly falling myself before I realized that I needed to focus on the path in front of me to keep from falling into the abyss.

"Suzanne? Is that you?"

I played my beam over the woman standing there on the edge of the hillside. It was Nicole.

"What happened? Are you okay?"

"It's Hank. He fell," she said, the sobs pouring out of her. Grace joined us before I could ask her anything else, and then the others approached us in the darkness.

"What happened, Nicole? Did he try to push you?" I asked her.

She shook her head, dispelling the notion that Hank was the person trying to kill her. "Someone shoved me from behind! I couldn't see who it was. All I saw was a glimpse of one of the hoodies we got today. Hank was right there, trying to save me! He must have thought something was odd, and he was following me to make sure that I was okay. Anyway, I felt him grab me at the last second to keep me from going over the hillside, but he slipped instead. I tried to save him, but I couldn't! Do you think he's okay?"

Grace cautiously approached the edge and played her flashlight beam down below. When I looked at her face, she held her light up, and I could see a pretty grim expression as she shook her head from side to side.

Evidently Hank was far from okay.

"Nicole, this is important," I said. "Is there *anything* you can tell us about who might have pushed you?"

Through her tears, she said, "I couldn't see! My light went out the moment I got shoved, and all I saw was Hank's light falling as it flew out of his hands. It took a long time for it to go out."

"Where were you all just now?" I asked as I played my light over the other people in our party, who had all joined us by then.

Janelle said, "I was in the restroom in our cottage. When I heard the commotion, I came out to see what was going on."

"Can you prove that?" Georgia asked her cuttingly.

"I was alone, if that's what you mean. Where were you?"

"I was sneaking around out in back of the lodge having a smoke," she said.

"Smoking's not allowed on the resort property," Janelle protested.

"Thus the sneaking." She pointed her light at Celia. "Where were you?"

"I was out at the gazebo, looking for stars," she said.

I looked up at the sky, still dense with clouds. "There aren't any out tonight."

"That's why I started back when I heard the first scream." She went to her sister as though she just realized that comforting her was what she should have been doing all along instead of hanging back in the shadows. "Are you okay, Sis?"

"No, not really," Nicole said shakily. At least she'd stopped crying for the moment, but I had my doubts if the hiatus would last very long.

"That just leaves you, Dina," I said.

"I was in the kitchen trying to find another piece of pie,"

she confessed. "I'm not proud of it, but I was still a little hungry after the meal, and it was awfully good."

"Did anyone see you there?" I asked her.

"No, I was by myself." Dina pointed her light at Grace. "Where were you, by the way? And how about you, Suzanne? You're asking us for alibis. It's only fair that we hear yours."

She was correct; it was only fair. I'd asked them about their whereabouts. Why shouldn't they have the same right to know where we were? "I was just leaving the cottage, getting ready to come back to the lodge to see what was going on after I couldn't sleep," I said.

Grace replied, "I was at my car looking for something to make notes with," she said. "Nicole's been sharing some new ideas with me, and I wanted to get them down on paper before I forgot everything."

"So, no one can alibi anyone else," I said. "That's just perfect." I suddenly realized that we, as guests, were all alone. "Where's the staff? Shouldn't they have heard us by now and come running?"

Grace explained to me, "That's right. You missed the announcement. The hostess here just had her baby, and everybody left to go into town to see her after we all finished eating. They'll be back first thing tomorrow morning."

"We can't wait that long for them," I said. "Somebody needs to drive into town and get the police out here, pronto." Just as I said it, cold, icy rain began pouring down from the sky. The lodge's porch was the closest refuge that would hold all of us, so we ran for cover together. "Where did that come from all of a sudden?" Celia asked.

"It's been overcast all day," Georgia replied. "I'm surprised that it took this long to finally start raining."

"Is there some snow mixed in as well?" Janelle asked us as she stuck her hand out.

"It's cold enough, so anything's possible," I said as the first crack of lightning struck, much too close to us. "Maybe we should all go inside until this storm passes."

"What about Hank? We can't just leave him there!" Nicole said. While her sentiments were admirable, I'd taken a peek over that edge myself after Grace had, and judging from the odd way the man's neck was turned, I had a feeling that he was beyond any help we could give him ever again.

"It's the best we can do at the moment," I said as another lightning bolt struck, filling the air just before a strong smell of ozone materialized. I happened to be looking toward the entrance where we'd driven up a handful of hours earlier, and I saw a brilliant flash of light struck the mighty oak I'd noticed earlier. Bark exploded from the trunk as the bolt struck home, setting the tree on fire despite the downpour. It seemed to split it in half right before my eyes, leaving two sides of the massive oak plummeting to the ground, shaking the earth under our feet as each piece landed harshly.

I was about to go see if we could still get around it when Grace put a hand on my shoulder. "Nobody leaves until this storm is over; not even you, Suzanne."

I appreciated the sentiment, but I knew that if we couldn't get off that mountain, every last one of us but one would be stuck there with a killer.

CHAPTER 10

A DDING INSULT TO INJURY, AS the storm finally began to let up, there was one last lightning strike close to home. We all heard the explosion and, almost instantaneously, the following deafening clap of thunder. At that instant, every single light went out in the lodge, and everywhere else in the resort, for that matter.

We'd lost power, and at the worst possible moment as the temperature really started to drop. Could we get all snow after all? I hoped not. We had enough obstacles without the burden of dealing with a winter wonderland on the mountaintop.

It felt as though the heavy precipitation had lasted forever, but with the last burst of lightning and thunder, it suddenly began to let up, petering out into the distance as the storm moved away, assaulting the next area along the line.

Once I finally felt it was safe to leave, I headed off the porch as Grace asked me, "Where are you going?"

"I have to see how bad the road is," I said. "Like I said before, it's urgent that someone drives to the nearest town and gets help."

"I'm coming with you, then," Grace said.

"We all will," Nicole answered.

"I'm not going out there in the dark," Celia complained. "Who knows what's out there?"

"You're coming with us, Celia," her sister said firmly, and then she turned to the rest of our little group. "And so are you all. The only way that any of us can be absolutely sure that we're safe is to stick together from here on out."

Nicole was clearly the boss, and she was acting like it. Though she had no real control over Celia or Dina or even me, for that matter, they agreed as well. Most likely they didn't want to be left alone with a possible killer, or perhaps they were just taking the path of least resistance. Either way, I was eager to see what that tree had done to our chances of escape.

By dying in such a spectacular fashion, the old oak had effectively blockaded us from the outside world. I couldn't imagine cutting through it with a normal-sized chainsaw, even if I knew how to operate one, which I didn't. I was guessing that it would take a full crew to cut it up and move it out of the way, and I had a feeling that it would have to be done from the other side of the road. When the tree had fallen, it had also loosened a portion of the road beneath it, which had then been subject to the pouring precip we'd experienced after the initial lightning strike. There was a chasm where the road used to be, ten feet of gravel that had simply dropped down into the abyss without a trace.

No one would be leaving the Shadow Mountain Resort any time soon, at least not in a vehicle.

"Some of us could probably walk it," Janelle suggested as we all played our beams over the gaping expanse.

"Seven miles? With who knows what we could encounter on the way down the mountain? Use your head, Janelle," Georgia snapped.

"It was just a thought," she said.

Celia surprised me by patting her arm. "Don't feel bad. I was thinking the exact same thing."

"Clearly, none of us are going anywhere," I responded. "We're just going to have to all make the best of it until someone comes for us."

"I'm cold," Dina said. "Shouldn't we go back to our rooms?

I'm going to hate staying at that lodge all by myself, since you are all in cottages."

"You're not going to have to," I spoke up. "When I said that we needed to stick together, I meant it. I don't know about the rest of you, but Grace and I are moving our things up to the lodge immediately. We'll all sleep in the main reception area, since there enough couches for all of us. After all, we've got a fireplace there, and there's plenty of room. It might not be the most comfortable sleep of your life, but at least we should all make it through the night."

"That sounds like a solid plan to me," Nicole said, defying anyone to contradict her. I was happy to have both Grace and her on my side. "We're all going to do exactly as Suzanne has suggested. We'll stop at the cottages and collect our things, and then we're all heading to the lodge, together."

That's what we did, stopping just long enough at Pine, Spruce, Fir, and Hemlock to collect our things before we made our way back to the lodge, our bags in tow.

As we walked into the main reception area, Georgia said, "There has to be a generator here, given how secluded this place is. Shouldn't we try to find it?"

"Would you know how to operate it even if we did?" Dina asked her.

"It can't be that difficult," she said. "What do you think, Nicole?"

"While I like the idea of having power, maybe it should wait until morning. There are plenty of blankets here, and we've got a massive fireplace to keep us warm and toasty. Why don't we deal with that tomorrow? The last thing we need is someone stumbling around in the dark and getting hurt, too."

"Someone else, you mean," I added under my breath, just loud enough for Grace to hear it.

She nodded, and I could see the dire expression on her face in the firelight.

"Tell you what. Let's break up into pairs and gather what we can from the rooms," Nicole said. "Celia, you come with me. Grace, why don't you and Suzanne stick together? Janelle, you and Georgia should team up, and why don't you take Dina with you, while you're at it?"

"I'd rather go with you and Celia, if you don't mind," Dina said.

"If you must. Remember, this is going to be a quick scouting mission. Find what you think we can use, and then hurry back here."

We had all started to leave when Nicole motioned to me. "Suzanne, do you and Grace have a second?"

"Sure," I said, as Grace and I joined her by the fire. "What's up?"

"Keep your eyes open. Whoever tried to kill me might take another shot at it, given how helpless we all are right now."

"There's safety in numbers," I said. "Honestly, I'm glad that Dina's going with you and Celia."

"Do you still think my sister might have done it?" Nicole asked me.

"I don't know, but if there are two other people with you, there's less chance that someone's going to try something. It probably wouldn't hurt if Grace and I went with you, too."

"Thanks, but we need to stick with the original plan. Don't worry. It will be fine."

I had to wonder if Hank had thought the same thing just before he'd been shoved over the edge of the path, tumbling far below to his probable death, but I decided not to bring that up. I was fairly certain that it was in the forefront of Nicole's thoughts anyway. "See you soon, then," I said.

The moment Grace and I were away from the others, she asked me softly, "Do you honestly think this is such a good idea?"

"Maybe not, but it will take forever if we don't break up at least a little. Hey, where are you going?"

"I'm looking for the supply closet," Grace said as she began opening doors near the front desk. "This resort offers hikes and even overnight camping, so they have to have supplies. Sleeping bags and air mattresses might be nice to have tonight. Did you feel the way the temperature was falling when we were outside? Even with the fireplace going full blast, we still might be in for a chilly night."

We found the supply closet after three tries, and it was a veritable gold mine. Not only were there enough sleeping bags for all of us, but there were tiny lanterns as well, all solar and crank charged, I was happy to see. Grace and I moved them out into the main area by the fireplace, rearranged some of the furniture so we could all be close to the fire, and then we waited for the others. I decided that the fire needed a little more fuel, so I threw a pair of logs onto it, watching the sparks fly as the wood landed. "There, that should help a little."

"At least we have enough wood," Grace said. "Did you see how much was stacked out front on the porch?"

"We'll never burn through that, but even if we do, there's some extra at each cottage, too." I looked around, but no one had rejoined us yet. "Speaking of firewood, someone used a piece to try to give Nicole a very bad headache tonight."

"What happened?"

After I told her about the booby-trapped door, Grace said, "Somebody wants that woman dead, don't they?"

"I wouldn't trade places with her on a bet, myself," I said. "The question is, who's behind all of these attempts, and who killed Hank?"

"From the way Nicole told the story, Hank's fall wasn't planned. He got shoved out of the way; nobody pushed him on purpose."

"Maybe that's so, but he was trying to keep Nicole from suffering the same fate that he did, so as far as I'm concerned, it's just as much a murder as though whoever had done that had shoved Hank over that cliff herself."

"I can't believe how well Nicole is holding it together," Grace said. "If I were in her position, I'd be hiding in the corner somewhere crying my eyes out."

"I doubt it. Knowing you, you'd arm yourself with something lethal and dare the killer to try again," I said as I patted her shoulder.

"I can't stop thinking about poor Hank. He could be a real jerk sometimes, but at least he died saving someone else. I suppose in a way, that makes him a hero."

"What people say matters, but what they do matters even more," I said in agreement.

"What should we do about Nicole?" Grace asked me.

"The only thing we can do. We need to keep an eye on her, and that includes all night tonight."

"Are you saying that we should stay awake and guard her around the clock?"

"Yes, but not so overtly. Tell you what. If you can stay awake until one, I can handle the rest of the night. After all, I'm used to those hours anyway."

"Are you sure?" Grace asked me.

"Positive. As soon as the others come back, I'm bedding down over there," I said as I pointed to one of the couches away from the fire. I'd already put one of the sleeping bags on it.

"Are you sure you wouldn't rather have one of the couches closer to the fire?" Grace asked me.

"No, let everyone else fight over those spots. I'll be fine over there."

Georgia and Janelle came back with pillows and blankets,

while Nicole, Celia, and Dina brought bottled waters and a few snacks from the kitchen.

Once everyone was settled in, I said, "If you'll all excuse me, I'm going to get a little rest."

"How can you sleep after all that's happened?" Georgia asked me.

"It's easy. I just close my eyes and count jumping donuts," I said.

It might have helped if everyone there had known that I was a donutmaker by trade, but I didn't care enough to explain myself. Instead, I crawled into the sleeping bag I'd claimed earlier, keeping my clothes on to stay warm, and then I nodded off to sleep.

The next thing I knew, Grace was shaking my shoulder. Had I overslept? No, my internal clock told me that I still had a few more minutes of rest. "What's wrong?"

"Nothing. I need to pee, though," she said. "I held it as long as I could, but I've really got to go."

"Would you like me to go with you?" I asked her groggily.

"No thanks, I've been doing it by myself since kindergarten," she said.

"I meant to be safe," I said as I stood and stretched. I'd slept surprisingly well, given the circumstances and the conditions.

"What do I have to be afraid of?" She gestured around us. "Everyone else is fast asleep."

"Go on, then," I said.

I could see that it was true. The rest of our party was still soundly sleeping, and a few of the ladies were even snoring. It amused me when I saw that Georgia and Dina had taken the two couches closest to the fire. Did that make them the alpha females, or was Nicole stronger by giving up a comfy spot to one of the others? I wasn't sure, but I knew that I'd have a little time to consider the possibilities while I was playing guard dog. I added another log to the fire and felt the heat on my hands and cheeks. I wasn't sure what we would have done without the fireplace, and I was glad to have it. In a way, it reminded me of the cottage that I shared back in April Springs with my husband, and I wondered what Jake was doing at that very moment. Sound asleep, no doubt, unaware of the trouble his wife was currently in. If he'd had any idea, I knew without question that he'd be fighting his way up that mountain, no matter the danger or the cost, to get to me. But with the lack of a cellphone signal and no outside lines, there was no way that he'd know that I wasn't up here having the time of my life.

Grace came back a minute later, and I was glad for her presence. "Thinking about Jake?" she asked me as she joined me by the fire.

"As a matter of fact, I was. How did you know?"

"It's not hard. You get this goofy smile on your face whenever you think about him."

I laughed softly. "I didn't realize I was that transparent."

"It's not a bad thing, Suzanne." She yawned once, and then she asked, "Would you like some company?"

"Go to bed, Grace. I'll see you in the morning."

"Good night," she said, and soon enough, I heard her soft snores, blending in with the others as though they were members of some slumbering choir.

I pulled one of the overstuffed chairs closer to the fire and found a place where I could watch both the flames and everyone else while I was at it. I knew that most children looked like little angels when they slept, but I wasn't sure I could say that about this crew. That might have been more from the weird flickering shadows the firelight threw out or the ages of my group, but none of them looked particularly innocent at the moment, even Grace. They weren't even all that peaceful, either, if their expressions were any indication. Most of them appeared to be battling their own personal demons, and I was glad that I couldn't see into any of their dreams.

No matter how I considered it, I knew that I was in for a long night.

CHAPTER 11

W HEN THE SUN FINALLY CAME up, it seemed brighter than it should have been to me. Had my eyes been that sensitized to the lack of light? Puzzled, I stood, stretched, and then I moved over to one of the windows. Peering outside, I suddenly realized why we were being bathed in so much light.

Sometime when the rest of the world had been sleeping, we'd been visited by a silent snowstorm.

From the look of things outside, we had a new problem to contend with, as if having a killer among us wasn't enough.

"Is that really snow?" Celia asked me over my shoulder. "Seriously?"

"It looks serious enough to me," I said softly. "We need to keep it down. The rest of them are all sleeping." I glanced over at Grace and saw that she was awake, but she clearly didn't want Nicole's sister to know that.

"I'm hungry," she said plaintively.

"Then why don't we go in the kitchen and see about getting us all something to eat?" It was the perfect opportunity to get her alone. I still had a hard time believing that Celia would try to kill her sister, but what did I know?

"Fine by me," she said.

I headed off for the connecting door between the dining room and the kitchen, with Celia just behind me. Grace frowned at me, looked at Celia, and then at Nicole. I shrugged, because what else could I do? My plan the night before for all of us to stay together was not going to be tenable today. Bathroom breaks alone would be a nightmare, but I stood by my buddy-system idea. If the whole crew knew which teams were coupled, then if Nicole ended up dead, we'd be able to pinpoint the killer, barring the off chance that two of them were trying to get rid of her and were conspiring to commit the murder together. Frankly, I didn't think that was possible, given the level of disharmony they were all showing. In my mind, there was no way that any of them was that good at acting.

Celia and I went from the dining room into the kitchen, and the first thing I did was check the stovetop. If it was electric, we were going to be eating cold food until someone was able to dig us out of there. I was relieved to find that the stovetop was hooked up to propane, though, because I got an instant blue flame when I turned it on. Finally, at least something was going our way.

"What are we having?" Celia asked me.

"If you can wait, how about some donuts?"

"Do you know how to make them?" she asked me.

"I guess you haven't heard. That's what I do for a living."

"Seriously?" she asked me, and for the first time since we'd met, I saw a little spark of light in her eyes. "That is really cool."

"I don't know about that. The hours are dreadful, the pay works out to be less than minimum wage, but on the plus side, I'm my own boss, and I make people happy with what I provide them. All in all, it's a pretty sweet deal."

"I'll bet it is," Celia said. "Was it hard to learn how to do?"

"Maybe at first, but it's like anything else. After a while, I managed to get the hang of it." There was a great deal more to it than that, but it was all the explanation Celia needed.

"I think it sounds like a blast." She hesitated a moment, and then she asked, "Suzanne, could you teach me how to do it?"

"Why not?" What could it hurt? If it helped to let her guard down, maybe she'd tell me something inadvertently.

"Excellent. What should we do first?" Celia asked me. The change in her was so dramatic I almost had a hard time believing that she wasn't putting me on, but one glance at her face told me that she was genuinely interested.

"Let's see what kind of ingredients we can find on hand," I said as I went to the massive refrigerator. There was no danger of anything spoiling for quite some time, since the warmth from the fireplace two rooms away couldn't reach where we were working. Still, it would be a good idea to get in and out. "As I hand you things, put them on the counter behind you."

"I can do that," she said.

I opened the door, and in quick succession, I grabbed a massive tub of sour cream, a few eggs, and some whole milk.

"That can't be all that you need," she said doubtfully.

"That's all of the wet ingredients, except for the sugar."

"Sugar isn't wet, though, is it?" Celia asked.

"It combines so easily with moisture that it's classified that way in most recipes." Grabbing one of the large mixing bowls hanging from hooks above my head, I measured out two cups of milk and then followed it up with a cup of sour cream. After that, I put the containers back into the refrigerator.

"Now let's raid the pantry," I told her.

"What do we need besides sugar?"

I was using one of my most basic recipes, the one I'd first learned to make donuts myself, as a matter of fact, and I'd made it so many times that it had been committed to memory. When I'd had my recipe book stolen and burned once a long time ago, before I got a copy from Sharon Blake, it was my fallback donut I'd prepared while I'd searched for my way back. Before I walked into the pantry, I grabbed another mixing bowl, along with cup, tablespoon, and teaspoon measuring devices. Scanning the shelves, I collected sugar, bread flour, baking soda, nutmeg, cinnamon, and salt and put the containers on the center island in the pantry. It was a nice space, and I envied the chefs there, but not for long. I had donuts to make.

"Now we measure out and mix the dry ingredients," I said.

"I really would like to help," she said.

"Have you ever baked before?"

"A little," she admitted, which probably meant not much, if any, at all.

"Why don't you help me when it's time to cut the donut rounds out of the dough? How does that sound?"

"Can I be the one who bakes them?"

"These will be fried, not baked, and there's an art to putting them in without burning yourself in the process."

She clearly hadn't realized there was any danger involved in the process. "Fine. I'll watch."

"Good," I said as I started measuring out ingredients and adding them to the new bowl, calling out the names and quantities as I worked. "In the bowl, I'm adding eight cups of bread flour, two cups of granulated sugar, two teaspoons of baking soda, two teaspoons of cinnamon, two teaspoons of nutmeg, and finally, four or five dashes of salt."

"How much is a dash?" she asked me.

"Pretend you have a salt shaker in your hand. Shake it quickly over the bowl, and that's going to be about one dash."

"I thought the sugar was a wet ingredient," she said plaintively.

"It is, but for this recipe, it goes in with the dry ingredients." I grabbed the cup measurement and took another quantity out of the flour bin. "That's it. Let's go back out into the kitchen."

"What's that for?"

"You'll see," I said. Last, I spotted some peanut oil in a big container with a spout for easy pouring. "Grab another bowl for me, would you?"

She looked pleased to be helping and came back a minute later. I handed her the bowl I'd mixed the dry ingredients in. "Take this back out front, and be careful not to spill any of it."

"Should I go ahead and add in the wet stuff to it?"

"Don't do anything until I get there," I said.

"Fine. I was just asking."

I tried to soften my voice. "Celia, believe it or not, there's a real art to it, which I'll teach you after I get the oil."

"What do we need oil for?"

"It's what we're going to fry the donuts in," I said.

That seemed to satisfy her, and after I drew a sufficient amount of oil, I rejoined her in the kitchen, hoping that she hadn't disobeyed me and started without me.

She hadn't, to my relief.

I took out a nice pot from storage, added the peanut oil, and then put it on the stovetop, turning it to high. While the oil was heating, I took a smaller bowl, broke open and beat the eggs, then I added it to the dry mix that I'd made up in the pantry, holding that last cup of flour out of the mix. Once I had the consistency I liked, I added the milk and sour cream, folding it all in lightly with a whisk. It still needed a little flour, so I tipped a touch in, and Celia nodded knowingly. After kneading it gently for a minute, I touched the dough with two fingers, and nothing stuck to them. The consistency felt right to me, so I floured the countertop and then put the ball of dough in the center. Taking a French rolling pin, I rolled it out until it was around a quarter inch thick.

"Now, we need a donut cutter. Would you look through the drawers and see if you can find one?"

"What's it look like?" she asked me.

"I don't mean to be flippant, but it resembles something that would cut a donut from dough."

"What if they don't have one?" she said a minute after searching.

"We improvise," I said. Grabbing two different-sized glasses, I powdered their edges with flour and pressed down with the larger of the two.

"I thought I was going to get to help," she said.

"Sorry. I forgot. You can cut out the holes, but I'll lift them, okay?"

"Okay," she said. As I worked, Celia followed behind me with the smaller glass, cutting out holes from the circles I'd created. Using the point of a knife, I flicked the holes out and then pulled out enough rounds to start the first batch. The temperature of the oil was up to 375 degrees F, so we were ready to get started.

"Celia, did you happen to see a slotted spoon while you were looking in the drawers?"

She retrieved it quickly, a proud look on her face. After I took it from her, I said, "Now, take one of those wire cooling racks and put it on the counter, but first put down some paper towels to catch the extra oil."

I slid the first four rounds into the oil, being careful not to splash, and started to wait.

"How long do they take?"

"Two minutes on each side," I said.

"Nicole never let me help her in the kitchen. Thanks for including me."

"You two aren't that close, are you?"

Celia shrugged. "The truth is that we've never really gotten along. She was bossy growing up, and none of that has changed now that we're adults."

"Do you resent her being in control of your money?"

Celia frowned at me. "How did you know about that?"

I shrugged. Had I just made a tactical error tipping my hand? "I didn't realize that it was supposed to be a secret. Sorry."

"It's not your fault. I honestly don't care who knows. I just can't wait until next week."

"What happens then?" I asked her, stopping long enough to flip the donuts. They were nicely browned, and I was happy with the results.

"I get my money. All of it," she said. "Nicole has control of it now, but that all ends on my birthday."

So maybe the motive we'd assigned Celia hadn't been valid after all. If she just had to wait a week to get control of her inheritance, there was no reason for her to try to kill her sister.

"Well, let me say it early: happy birthday," I said.

"Thanks." She looked into the pot. "Are we eating those plain?"

"We could make icing or just use powdered sugar dusted on top," I said. "Which way do you prefer?"

"Let's do icing. It looks so cool, don't you think?"

"As a matter of fact, I do," I said. "Would you mind grabbing the powdered sugar for me in the pantry?"

"Happy to," she said.

By the time she was back, the first four donuts were finished, out and cooling on the rack, and the next four were in the hot oil.

"How hard is the icing to make?"

"We're doing the easy version," I said. I measured out some powdered sugar, added a touch of vanilla extract I'd found, and then enough cold water to make a slurry from it all.

"That's it?" she asked. "Can I taste it?"

"Why not?" I put a little on the tip of a spoon and handed it to her.

She smiled brightly after she tasted it. "It's perfect."

"Wait until you've had a donut with it," I said.

Just then, the kitchen door opened, and the entire crew walked in.

"We smelled food," Grace said. "Are you actually making donuts? This wasn't supposed to be a busman's holiday, Suzanne."

"I don't mind," I said as I drizzled icing on the first four donuts.

Georgia tried to grab one, but I kept her at bay with the slotted spoon. "Celia gets the first one, since she helped me make them."

The woman looked as though she'd just won a prize, and after quick consideration, she chose the one with the most icing. After taking a bite, she smiled broadly. "They are absolutely delicious."

"I'm next," Georgia said, and she grabbed one as well. Janelle and Dina took the last two, and I could see that Nicole and Grace were a little disappointed at being left out. "Don't worry, there's more on the way soon."

After the donuts and holes were all fried and served, I nibbled on a few holes while Janelle and Nicole did the dishes. I hadn't protested too hard when they'd offered, and though we'd had to heat the water on the stovetop, everything was clean and back in order before long.

"Now that breakfast is over, we really should decide what to do next," Nicole said to the group. "I'm open to suggestions, everyone."

"I still think that we should send someone for help," Janelle said.

"On foot, through the snow, seven miles, and all of it downhill? Thanks, but no thanks," Georgia said.

"Aren't there any phones at the resort? There has to be a landline somewhere," I said.

"I checked it already," Nicole said. "The storm must have taken the line out as well."

"Has anyone tried different places on the property to see if we can get a signal on our cellphones?" Grace asked.

"It's awfully cold out there to be taking a casual stroll," Dina said.

I needed a chance to tell Grace what I'd learned from Celia, so I said, "I think it's a great idea. As a matter of fact, I'll go with you, Grace."

"Are you sure that's wise, Suzanne?" Nicole asked me.

"Don't worry about us. After all, we'll be together. Nothing's going to happen. Are you ready, Grace?"

My best friend seemed a little reluctant about the chilly stroll, but finally, she agreed.

Once we were bundled up in nearly everything we'd brought and standing outside the front door together, Grace said, "Let's be clear about something. Just because I suggested this idea doesn't mean that I was the one who wanted to do it."

"It's not going to work, anyway," I told her. "I tried to get a signal yesterday while I was touring the grounds so I could call Jake, but I couldn't get through anywhere."

"Then why are we out here in the freezing cold?" Grace asked me.

"We need to talk, and I figured this was the best way to get a little privacy," I said.

After I brought her up to date on what Celia had told me while I'd made breakfast, Grace nodded. "You've still got it, don't you?"

"What do you mean?"

"Suzanne, you always could get people to open up to you. At least now we can take one name off our list."

"Only if it's true. Besides, it's still too early to celebrate," I said. "We still have Dina, Georgia, and Janelle on our suspect list."

"Three is always better than four unless we're talking about donuts," she said, rubbing her hands together furiously. "How long do we have to keep up this charade?"

"A little bit longer, I think," I said.

"What do we do in the meantime?"

"I want to go back to Pine Cottage and see if there are any clues I missed yesterday as to who might have tried to get rid of Nicole. Are you game?"

"Lead the way," Grace said, and we trudged through the snow in search of something that might be able to tell us where to look next.

CHAPTER 12

"WHAT EXACTLY ARE WE HOPING to find?"
Grace asked me as we took our first steps off
the porch.

"If I knew that, we wouldn't have to look, now would we?"
I asked her with a grin. At that moment, I saw something that
sent chills through me, and I put a hand up to stop Grace.

"What is it? What's wrong, Suzanne?"

"Look," I said as I pointed at the freshly fallen snow just
behind the overhang of the veranda's roof.

There were footprints in it, leading toward the cottages.

The problem with that was, at least in theory, none of us had
left the lodge all morning.

CHAPTER 13

"**I**s SOMEONE ELSE UP HERE?" Grace asked me as she quickly looked around us.

"How can it be anything *but* a stranger among us?" I asked her as I studied the prints. "If you weren't watching the group, then I was. Nobody could just take off on their own and start exploring without at least *one* of us knowing about it."

"I'm afraid that's not entirely true," Grace said softly.

"What do you mean?"

"Suzanne, once everyone was awake, they all scattered looking for bathrooms. I couldn't keep track of everyone at the same time. You were making donuts in the kitchen, so I couldn't get you to help me watch every last one of them. I'm afraid it could have been any one of them, except Celia, of course, since she was with you."

It was clear that she felt bad about it. "Grace, it's not your fault. I just assumed the buddy system we put in place last night would still be working this morning."

"Getting this group to follow rules is like trying to herd cats," she said.

"So these could have been made by just about any one of us after all," I said as I looked more closely at the nearest print. Though it was still quite cold out, the sun had already begun to melt the snow, and the tread marks had partially thawed into obscurity as to specific ways to identify their maker. I put my foot inside one of the prints for scale, but that wasn't really any help, since there was no way I could know how small it had started. I glanced back at the lodge, but no one was watching us, though I could see the window I'd peered out earlier clearly enough. "At least we can be pretty sure that it was one of us," I said as I stood fully erect.

"How could you possibly know that?"

"I can't be positive, but I believe that I would have noticed if there had been tracks in the snow when I first looked out this morning."

"That doesn't necessarily mean that we weren't visited later while you were busy in the kitchen." She frowned a moment before adding, "Suzanne, there's something else we need to consider."

"What's that?"

"What if Hank really isn't dead, and he somehow managed to climb up that embankment last night?"

It was a sobering thought. "You saw the way his neck was positioned. Is it really possible to fake that?"

"We didn't have very good light," Grace said, "and besides, he was pretty far away. Maybe we were wrong."

"Why wouldn't he join us at the lodge if that were the case?" I asked her.

"If you'd tried to prevent a murder and ended up being the accidental victim yourself, would you rush back to be with the killer?"

"I honestly don't know what I'd do in those circumstances."

"Let's see how close these footprints come to the lodge," she said.

It was a good idea, so we tracked the steps away from the cottages, instead of the ones going toward them. Grace's hunch turned out to be a sound one.

There was a clear set of footprints that led straight up to the side entrance of the lodge.

"Suzanne, he must be inside!" Grace said. "We've got to tell everyone right now."

I put a hand on her shoulder, restraining her. "Take it easy and think about it. We don't know anything for sure yet, Grace. These footprints could easily have been someone coming and going, stepping in the same spots both ways."

"I still think we should check the lodge thoroughly," she insisted.

"I do, too, but it's going to have to wait."

"For what?"

"We need to see if Hank's body is at the bottom of that precipice or not," I replied.

"What if he's still down there?" she asked me with a shiver. "What do we do then?"

"We try to figure out who was out walking in the snow alone. They clearly had the same idea that we had to check on Hank's body. It's not hard to see that these prints head straight to the cottages from here and to the spot where your district manager fell."

Grace and I approached the edge carefully, but when I looked over the lip, I couldn't see anything out of place below; in particular, there were no dead bodies lying there. The snow must have collected and blown sometime during the night, because now there was enough of it down there that I couldn't tell if it was hiding Hank's remains or not. "Can you see anything?" I asked Grace.

"He's either not there, or the snow somehow covered him up," she said.

"I think he's still there," I answered after a minute of thought. "He must be."

"How can you say that? Did you see something that I missed?"

"It's not what I see, it's what I don't see," I told her.

"Leave the riddles to Hank, would you? I need you to be a little clearer with me."

"Look around," I said as I pointed to the slope below us. "Do you see *any* evidence that someone climbed out of there?"

Grace looked intently for a full minute, and then she finally glanced back at me and shook her head. "I don't see anything, but there's another possibility; he might have found another way up."

"That's true," I said, frowning at the thought. If those footprints did belong to Hank and he was now hiding somewhere in the lodge, I was afraid of what might happen next. It was pretty clear that he was in no rush to come forward, so that meant that he was lurking in the shadows, staying out of our way and hatching a plan for revenge of his own. I didn't want to be the person who had caused him to fall if that were the case.

"What do we do now?" Grace asked me.

"What can we do? We press on."

I took a step in the direction of the cottages, and Grace put a hand on my shoulder, stopping me. "Suzanne, is that really a good idea? I have a feeling that we should rejoin the others and postpone the rest of this until later."

"We still have to uncover what's really going on around here, and the only way to have a chance of doing that is to follow those footprints and see where they take us."

Grace frowned for a moment before she spoke again. "I know you're right. We can't just let this go. There's too much at stake. Come on. Let's investigate, but if we see a snowman along the way, I'm running back to the lodge. I'm just warning you ahead of time."

"I don't think it's going to happen, but if it does, I'll be right behind you," I said.

"Yeah, well, I didn't think we'd find footprints out here, either, but I was wrong about that, too, wasn't I?"

"There's got to be a logical explanation for it," I told her.

"Remind me of that when whoever we're following decides to kill us," she said.

Ignoring the lack of logic in her statement, I pressed on. I had to admit, though, having Grace beside me gave me a great deal more courage than I would have had if I'd been alone. There were more benefits to the buddy system than I'd first realized.

We got to the Hemlock cottage first. "Is there even any reason to go inside?" Grace asked me. "I can say with a fair amount of certainty that neither one of us has been plotting to kill Nicole over the past few weeks."

"You never know," I said as I opened the door and peered inside.

"Thanks for the vote of confidence," Grace said.

"That's not what I meant, and you know it. Someone could have considered this a safe place to stash something incriminating. That way, if we happened to find it, we wouldn't know who to blame for it."

"I like the way you think," she said. "Devious and all, I mean."

"Coming from you, I'll take it for the compliment I'm sure that you meant it to be," I said as I looked around the small room. It was quick work pulling open the drawers, lifting the mattresses, checking the bathrooms, and scanning the small space for anywhere someone could hide something.

"There's nothing here that doesn't belong," Grace said.

"I knew that it was a long shot, but we had to check," I replied. "Now let's go see what Fir has to hold."

"Who was in Fir again?" she asked me as we walked through the snow to the next stone cottage.

"That's where Georgia and Janelle were supposed to stay," I told her. "Those two seem to have a real distinct dislike for each other, don't they? Or is it just me?"

"No, you read the situation correctly," Grace answered. "It was bad enough before Hank started playing his little mind games, but since he offered the promotion as a prize, they've been openly hostile toward one another."

"What about with Hank?" I asked her.

"What do you mean?"

"Did either one of them show any animosity toward your boss?"

"Certainly not openly, but I know that both women were unhappy with the way he was running things."

"I wonder," I said, and then I failed to follow it up.

"What exactly are you wondering about?" she asked me.

"What if Nicole hadn't been the target after all?" I asked. "Could one of them have meant to send Hank plummeting over the edge on purpose?"

Grace paused a moment before answering. "What good would it do either one of them to kill him? Nobody's getting promoted to his old job, not even Nicole. There are going to be some big changes if Hank is really dead, and I don't think anybody will be very excited about them. Besides, what about the earlier attempts on Nicole's life? As far as I know, nobody's had the nerve to come after Hank."

"Yes, of course. You're right. I was just thinking out loud."

"Don't stop doing it on my account. Sooner or later, we might just find the answer we're looking for that way."

Since Georgia and Janelle had removed their things from the Fir cottage, it felt as though we were striking out twice in a row with our inspections—that was, until Grace called out to me from one of the bedsides.

"What did you find?" I asked. She pulled out a single

printed sheet from behind the headboard, a place that I'd failed to examine in the cottage that we'd been slated to share. "Did you check that space behind the beds in Hemlock, too?"

"Yes, but this one's got pay dirt."

"What does it say?" I asked her as I moved closer.

"It's a sales report from our company. Hang on a second," she said as she studied it a little more intently. After a few moments, she was still frowning at the document, but unlike me, she hadn't been sharing her thought process aloud.

"What does it mean, though, Grace?"

"It looks legit at first glance, but someone faked it to make it look real. See the numbers in this column? They always line up on the ones I get. Not here, though."

I saw what she was talking about. "Okay, so it's been tinkered with. Why is the real question?"

Grace looked at the top of the sheet. "That's Nicole's employee number. The last two digits are transposed from mine, and I remember that we laughed about it when we saw how close they were once when they got mixed up."

"Why would someone fake one of her reports, though?"

"According to this sheet, she didn't win the job, at least not fair and square. The numbers just don't add up. See?"

She thrust the document toward me, so I took it and studied the entries. It could have been reporting the national debt for Lithuania for all that I knew. "I'll take your word for it."

"Suzanne, I'm willing to bet that either Janelle or Georgia was going to try to get Nicole fired this weekend. This is a pretty strong motive for murder, if you ask me."

"Nicole didn't kill anybody, though," I said. "How do you read it that way?"

"Maybe motive is the wrong word," she replied. "What if one of those two women tried to scare her into quitting by making a few clumsy attempts on her life? When that didn't work, they decided to come after her job directly. If Hank had seen this, it might have been tough for Nicole to explain it away, and knowing the man, I wouldn't have put it past him to fire Nicole and replace her with someone else on the spot, no matter how much she might protest that the report had been faked."

"But Hank never saw it, did he?" I asked.

"I doubt it, or we would have heard about it."

"The question is, whose headboard was it hidden behind, Georgia's or Janelle's?"

"It was the one for the bed closest to the front door, if that helps," Grace said.

"Why don't you hold onto it for now?" I asked her as I handed it back to her. "We might be able to use it later."

"How?" she asked me.

"I don't know, but the author doesn't know we have it, so there may be a way to make it useful. Is that it here?"

"As far as I can see," she said.

"Then let's move onto Hank's cottage, Spruce."

I'd expected it to be messy, but it was neat as a pin. We even went through the man's luggage, which gave me the creeps, but in the end, there was nothing there, at least not that we could use.

"Should we even bother going through Pine Cottage?" Grace asked me. "The potential victim and the one person we've come close to ruling out both stayed there."

"Just to be safe, let's look," I said.

There was nothing there, either, or it was too well hidden for us to find it.

I wasn't sure how to use the falsified sales report to our advantage yet, but it was time to go back to the lodge and tell the others at least some of the things we'd discovered so far.

CHAPTER 14

"How much of what we've found are we going to tell the group?" Grace asked me as we neared the lodge's front door.

"We definitely have to mention the footprints," I said.

"What about the sales report?"

"Let's keep that in reserve," I said. "Is that okay with you?"

"Hey, you're the boss of this investigation," she replied.

"I don't mean to be pushy about it," I said. "I just think it makes sense to wait, but if you believe otherwise, that's fine with me."

"No, I trust your instincts, Suzanne. Let's go in and see how people react to our news."

We found everyone gathered around the fireplace when we went back inside. Nicole didn't even wait for us to report. "What's wrong? What did you find out there?"

"There were footprints in the snow outside the lodge when we got out there," I said, trying to keep my voice calm.

"Sure, after you made them," Georgia replied.

"Hardly. We found these before we took our first step off the porch," Grace added.

"But we didn't see any this morning," Celia countered. "Suzanne, you and I both looked out the window." She moved there to check again. "Oh. I see them now."

"That's because they made them," Dina said.

"You're going to have to trust us. Someone else was outside before we went out," Grace said.

"Who would do that?" Nicole asked. "For what reason?"

"Maybe they were looking for something they accidently left behind in one of the cottages," I said. I didn't want to get into our theory that it might be Hank, coming back from his fall to exact punishment on whoever had made him tumble down the hillside.

"Like what?" Janelle asked.

"First, I'd like everyone to line up," I said.

"Why on earth should we do that?" Georgia asked in clear protest.

"We want to see if anyone's shoes are wet from the snow," I answered.

She immediately tucked her feet under her chair. "That's the most ludicrous thing I've ever heard in my life."

"If you weren't out skulking around in the snow, then you won't mind showing us," Grace said. "Only someone with something to hide would refuse to let us see their shoes."

"Fine. Happy?" Georgia asked as she brought both of her feet out. Her shoes were bone dry, as were everyone else's. It could mean one of three things, as far as I was concerned: none of them had ventured out before Grace and I had, meaning Hank might be in the lodge after all; whoever had done it had made sure to dry their shoes by the fire as soon as they got back; or there was indeed a stranger among us. I wasn't sure which option I preferred to be the truth.

"There's another theory," Grace said, "but I'm guessing that none of you are going to like it."

"Go on. We're listening," Nicole answered.

"We think it's a possibility that Hank is hiding somewhere in the lodge," she said.

I might have worded it differently, but it certainly had an immediate effect. Protests came from every direction until Nicole quieted everyone down. "Hold on. The least we can do is hear them out."

That stopped the protests, so I could speak in peace again. "We couldn't see any evidence of Hank's body when we looked over the cliff, and the footprints started, or ended, as the case might be, at the side entrance. He might have managed to climb up somewhere else, because we didn't see any evidence that he'd done it from where he went over. I'm not sure how likely it is that Hank would be able to recover from that fall, but if he did, he could be in the lodge, and I for one won't be able to rest until we've searched the place thoroughly."

I decided not to mention my theory that a stranger might be with us. There was no reason to drive tensions even higher unless I had some direct evidence to back that theory up.

There were nods of agreement from most of the others, but Janelle brought up something that we'd already considered ourselves. "If he survived the fall, why wouldn't he just walk up and come in through the front door?"

I'd been hoping that someone would ask that particular question. "We think it's possible that he might be looking for revenge on whoever tried to get rid of Nicole and shoved him over the edge instead."

Clearly, no one was happy about that particular theory. "Let's say for the sake of argument that you're right. What should we do about it?" Nicole asked us.

I shrugged. "I'm not the one in charge here, but if I were, I'd start searching the lodge from top to bottom, and while I was at it, I'd lock every door we came across."

"This place is massive," Dina said in frustration. "It's going to take forever."

"Not if we split up," I said. Grace and I weren't finished with our search for clues yet, and this would be a perfect opportunity to keep snooping inside the lodge while everyone else was occupied elsewhere. "Nicole, you and Celia can start in the attic and then take the second floor. Dina, you, Georgia, and Janelle can start in the basement, and Grace and I will take the first floor, unless anyone has any objections."

Nicole shook her head. "That sounds like a good plan. If Hank is indeed inside, the moment anyone sees him, scream at the top of your lungs, and the rest of us will come running. Is that agreed?"

Everyone nodded, and as they took the other levels, Grace and I made a cursory scan through the kitchen and pantry, and then we focused on the pile of bags we'd all gathered the night before.

"I feel funny searching through everyone else's things," Grace said as she picked a bag up at random.

"We have to do whatever we can to find out what's really going on here," I said as I grabbed a laptop bag.

"What if we get caught?" Grace asked me, clearly worried about the prospect.

"Then we plead ignorance and say that we were looking for our own things," I said. "What's this?" I'd glanced into the pocket of a laptop sleeve, and I'd found an official looking document. "Grace, come look at this."

She took it from me, scanned it, and then she said, "Does Dina think that Nicole's going to actually sign this?"

It was a waiver of liability absolving Dina for losing so much of Nicole's money.

I kept digging, and I hit pay dirt again. Buried deeper in the case's pocket were torn-up shreds of paper. I pieced several of them together on one of the nearby tables, with Grace helping me. It had to be one of the oddest jigsaw puzzles I'd ever done in my life.

"These are all Nicole's signatures," Grace said, frowning.

"Correction. I think they're attempts at forgery," I said.

"So if Nicole wasn't going to sign it willingly, then Dina was going to do it for her. That's ridiculous. Nicole would just deny that she'd ever signed it, and then where would Dina be?"

"What if Nicole wasn't around to set the record straight, though?" I asked.

Grace nodded in understanding. "If she'd been the one who'd tried to push Nicole over the edge, then no one would challenge the signature."

I took the waiver and the torn paper, and then I started to tuck them into my own bag for safekeeping. "That's the first place she'll look when she realizes that it's all gone," Grace said.

"What do you suggest we do with the evidence we've found, then?"

Grace moved over to the bulletin board and pulled on the glass door's handle. It opened to her touch, and she stashed everything we'd just found, along with the faked sales report, under a stack of old menus on display. I studied the case after she was finished, and I couldn't see where Grace had added anything to it at all. "That's clever. It's all hidden in plain sight."

"I have my moments," Grace said. "We've got some time left. Let's keep looking."

I grabbed another briefcase as she said, "There's no reason to bother with that one. I recognize it; it belongs to Nicole."

"Maybe so, but we still have to look at everything," I told her. On first inspection, it looked to be a random assortment of the type of paperwork a supervisor might have, but the last sheet was different from the rest. "Now that's interesting," I said.

"What did you find this time? Doesn't anyone store anything on their computers anymore? I haven't seen so much paper in my life."

"It appears to be an extension for the trust arrangement for Celia's money," I said.

"I'm not all that surprised you found something like that. Nicole has been worrying about her sister's spending habits for quite a while," Grace said.

"After talking to Celia earlier in the kitchen, I can say with certainty that there's no way she's going to ever sign anything like that, Grace. She wants her sister out of her finances. I don't know if it's wise or not, but that's really none of our business. That's between the two of them."

"Put it back, Suzanne. It's not a clue about the attempts on Nicole's life. All Celia has to do is refuse to sign it, and it's a moot point. We shouldn't be snooping in her stuff."

"Sorry," I said as I put the paper back where it belonged. At least I hoped that I did. Would Nicole notice if I hadn't gotten it exactly right? Chances are we were okay, given the random pattern of paperwork I'd found.

"There's nothing else here," I said finally as I put the last bag back in its place.

"That's enough, don't you think? With what we've found, we have reasons to suspect Dina, Georgia, and Janelle. That was our final grouping of suspects anyway."

"I just wish we knew who fabricated that sales report," I said.

A moment later, Nicole asked us from the doorway, "What exactly are the two of you up to, Grace? Suzanne, would either one of you care to answer me?"

The real question was how long had she been standing there, and exactly how much had she seen and heard before she'd spoken to us?

CHAPTER 15

"**A**RE YOU FINISHED WITH YOUR search so soon?" I asked her, stalling for time. "It's a pretty big place. We didn't expect anyone to be back this early."

"Clearly," Nicole said, with Celia standing just behind her. "Were you going through our things just now?"

"What? No. Of course not. I can't find my lip balm," I said. "I was searching my bag, and Grace was looking in hers for some I could borrow."

"No worries. I always carry a few spares," Celia said as she stepped forward and offered me a tube. "This dry air just kills my lips, too."

I took the offering, applied a healthy amount to my lips, and then handed it back to her. "Thanks so much."

"Keep it. I've got more in my bag," she said, which I knew for a fact was true, since I'd been the one who'd searched her things. That overabundance of lip balm was about the only thing out of the ordinary that she'd brought with her.

"Excellent," I said. "I take it you didn't have any luck finding Hank."

"We didn't, but who knows where he might be? For all we know, he might be hiding right under our noses, and we could have missed him, though I find it highly unlikely. You saw the way he was lying on the ground. There's no way he'd survive that fall."

"I'm afraid that I probably have to agree with you," I said, "but we still had to look. Funny, I wouldn't have pegged Hank as the heroic type."

"He certainly never displayed it while we were dating," she said, "but I knew that deep down, he still must have cared for me. Why else would he have sacrificed himself like that?"

"Since you've slept on it, do you have any new ideas as to who might have tried to shove you over the hillside last night?" Grace asked. "I know for me, sometimes things come back to me after a good night's sleep."

"I wish I could come up with something new, but it's still all just one big blur," Nicole said. "I'm deathly afraid that whoever did it is going to try again, though, especially since we're so isolated up here now."

"Don't worry, Sis. I'll watch your back," Celia said.

I wondered if she'd still feel that way if she knew what her sister was about to try to get her to sign, but I had no way to ask her without revealing that we'd been snooping in Nicole's things and had stumbled across the extension.

A moment later, Dina, Georgia, and Janelle came up from the basement. They all looked dusty and tired from their excursion. "The next time search parties go out, *we* get the upstairs," Georgia said. "That place was filthy."

"No sign of Hank, then?" I asked her.

"Did you *hear* a scream, Suzanne?" she asked sarcastically.

"To answer your question, no, we didn't see anything out of the ordinary on our search," Janelle supplied.

"How can we possibly say that, since we don't know what passes for ordinary around this gothic castle? It's a wonder they haven't filmed a horror movie here by now."

I decided to let her complaint pass for what it was: just another opportunity for Georgia to display her displeasure with the situation. She was in good company as far as that went. I wasn't particularly happy to be stuck at the lodge with a killer, either.

"I'm getting hungry," Janelle said. Then, almost apologetically, she added, "Not that your donuts weren't delicious this morning, but I need something a little more substantial for lunch."

I'd scanned the supplies earlier when I'd been gathering donut ingredients. "I suppose I could make us all sandwiches," I offered.

"How about grilled cheese?" Dina asked. "I don't mind grating a batch of cheddar for you."

"With ham, too," Georgia said.

"There are massive bags of chips in the pantry. I saw them when I was helping Suzanne earlier," Celia added.

"I suppose that I could get the drinks," Nicole offered.

"I'll get plates and linen napkins," Janelle said. "Hey, I've got an idea. Why don't we all eat in the kitchen? There's an island in the middle with enough stools to easily fit all of us. The dining room seems so stuffy."

"I'll help you with the place settings," Georgia said. It was next to the least she could do, but I didn't mind, since it was the only way that we'd all be together. She looked at my best friend and asked, "What are you going to contribute, Grace?"

"I'll be by Suzanne's side the entire time offering moral support," she said with a grin.

I wasn't exactly sure when I'd volunteered to be the head chef around the lodge, but at least I knew I could trust whatever I made. My specialties might not match the chef's or even my mother's, but I should be able to keep us fed until help arrived.

If it ever did, that was, and if anyone but the killer was left alive at the Shadow Mountain Lodge by the time they got there.

Lunch was good, even if I made that observation myself. The grilled ham and cheese sandwiches were tasty, with buttered bread toasted on a griddle I'd found in the kitchen, and it served its function perfectly, warming the ham as it melted the cheese, all the while giving the bread a good toasting. Nicole found sodas for us, Celia retrieved chips, and the kitchen island looked almost festive with the fine china on it. Georgia and Janelle had gone all out on the presentation, and I felt it was almost too fancy for the common food we ate. Still, given the circumstances, it turned out much better than we had any right to expect.

Until after the two pies I'd found were nearly completely consumed.

The period in which Georgia and Janelle were cooperating was clearly over when Georgia asked, "Are you going to eat *two* pieces of pie? I haven't had any yet."

Janelle put down the serving fork holding another healthy slab of cherry pie. "I'm sorry. I thought you were finished."

"I'll just bet you did," Georgia snapped as she grabbed the pie and placed it on a plate of her own. "That's your problem, Janelle; you're too greedy for your own good."

"I said I was sorry," she complained. "What more do you want from me?"

"I don't know, why don't you try admitting that you tried to rig the contest for Nicole's job in your favor?"

Janelle blushed a little from the accusation. "Hank found just as many shortcuts in your report as he did in mine."

"Isn't that water under the bridge at this point, ladies?" Nicole asked, trying to play the part of peacemaker.

"With all due respect, nothing's set in stone anymore, Nicole," Georgia said.

She looked surprised by the statement. "What do you mean by that?"

"Now that Hank's gone, don't you think the home office is going to reexamine how you got that job in the first place?" Georgia asked her.

"It's actually quite simple. I earned it," Nicole said icily. Had Georgia hit a nerve just then?

"So you say," Janelle replied. Were the two of them back to being allies again? It was enough to make my head spin, but I knew better than to interrupt them. Something valuable might come out of their squabbling if I just kept my mouth shut.

Unfortunately, Grace didn't have the same plan. "It's interesting that we're discussing sales reports. Suzanne and I happened to find something besides footprints on our walk this morning," she said.

I tried my best to signal her to drop it, but she either missed my clue or, more likely, chose to ignore it.

Janelle asked her, "What are you talking about?"

"Yes, I'd like to know that as well," Nicole added.

Georgia, for once in her life, was silent, but Dina wasn't. "Since I haven't been outside since we got here, I'd like to hear that myself." She was the only one who'd been planning to stay at the lodge out of all of us, though she hadn't chosen a room by the time we all joined up in the main reception area. Her bags had been intermixed with ours, thus allowing our earlier discovery. Hopefully Grace wouldn't bring that up, too, but I couldn't be sure at that point.

What choice did we have now but to show them what we'd found? I walked over to the bulletin board enclosure and took out the report we'd uncovered, leaving Dina's waiver and forgery attempts in place. As I tried to hand the sheet to Grace, I said, "Go on. Show them."

"Show us what?" Nicole asked.

"Give it to her instead, Suzanne," Grace instructed me, and I did as I was told.

Nicole's reaction was heated and instant. "This is all a lie!"

"What is it?" Georgia asked. Was she playing innocent, or did she really not know?

"It's a report stating that I falsified my numbers as well," Nicole replied.

"Don't worry," Grace said. "It's clearly a fake."

"How can you tell that?" Janelle asked. Was it a matter of personal wounded pride that she'd botched the attempt at fabrication, or was she sincerely curious? I wasn't getting anything from these two women.

"Look at the numbers in the last column," Grace said.

Nicole smiled for the first time since she'd learned that the report had surfaced. "The numbers don't align. I missed that myself. Where did you find this?"

"In the Fir cottage," I said.

Nicole turned to Janelle and Georgia. "Which one of you did this?"

"It wasn't me!" Janelle snapped.

"Don't look at me! I didn't do it, either!" Georgia answered nearly as quickly. She turned toward Janelle. "So that's what you were hiding when I came inside our cottage yesterday."

"I didn't hide anything," Janelle said. "Where did you find that?"

"Hang on a second," I said before Grace could supply the answer. This might be the wedge I'd been waiting for to break things open a little bit. "Georgia, exactly where did you see Janelle hiding something?"

"I didn't do anything!" Janelle insisted, nearly screaming this time.

"Please be quiet and let her speak," Nicole said.

"I don't know. It was somewhere around the beds. Was it under a mattress?"

Close, but no cigar. If Georgia had hidden it herself, she could be playing dumb with us. Then again, if she was innocent, that might be all the direction she could really give us.

"Sorry, but no," I said.

Janelle took my statement as full vindication, something I was nowhere near ready to award her. "See? I told you that I didn't do it."

"Where was it, then?" Janelle asked us.

Grace looked at me, and I nodded. "It was tucked behind one of the headboards," she said.

"Which one?" Georgia asked.

"Who had the bed farthest from the front door of the cottage?" I asked.

Janelle's face went ashen as Georgia crowed, "She did."

"Well, that was the headboard where we *didn't* find it, so it must have been yours," I told Georgia.

How quickly her victory turned to ashes. "Do you honestly think that means that I did it? Do you really think that I'm stupid enough to hide something that might incriminate me in my area and not someone else's?"

"We haven't figured out just how stupid you are yet," Janelle said smugly, clearly pleased with her shot at Georgia.

"Really? Is that how you want to try to spin this?" Georgia asked, whirling toward her roommate.

"Ladies! Enough!" Nicole silenced them, frowned at the report for a moment, and then folded it twice before tucking it into one of her pockets. I wanted it back, but it probably wasn't the best time to ask her for it. I'd get it later if I could find a way to justify making the request. I had a feeling that it had yielded its last clue, but I never knew with these things. "I believe it's time we retire to the reception hall. It's getting a bit chilly in here, wouldn't you all agree?"

I wasn't sure if she was talking about the air temperature or the interpersonal relationships, but either way, she was right. "Who is going to do dishes?" I asked. "I cooked, so I'm exempt."

I waited for one of them to dispute my right, and from my

resolute expression, they must have realized that asking me would be in vain.

"I'll do them," Dina said. "After all, none of this really concerns me. You all go on in, and I'll be along shortly."

I expected everyone to accept that offer, but Nicole wasn't interested. "No, I thought we agreed. We stay together from here on out."

"I suppose I could pitch in," Celia said.

I'd put a pot of water on full heat when we'd started eating, so at least we didn't have to wait for that. The resort must have had some kind of massive reservoir tank built overhead, because without electricity, there was no way to circulate the water.

Once the dishes were finished and put in the drying rack, we all headed out to the main room of the lodge where we'd spent the night before. I threw another log on the fire, and then I settled down on the couch beside Grace. If anything was going to happen, I wanted her to be close by when it did.

Everyone else took seats as well, with the exception of Nicole. She stood facing us, with her back to the fire. "It appears there are secrets here that need to see the light of day. I say we all put our cards on the table. After all, the only person who has anything to gain by silence is the killer. Are we agreed?"

It had been cleverly handled. Now no one could withhold information without putting a target on their backs. "Come now. Who wants to go first?" When no one spoke, Nicole smiled a little ruefully. "Very well. I'll get the ball rolling. I know some of you have reason to want to see me lose my new position, but don't you agree that killing me seems a little drastic? Which of you really feel as though you have any reason to want me to die?"

I got chills as she asked the question, and I doubted that I could have handled it that calmly if I'd been the one standing in front of that group.

"We all know that Celia had a reason," Dina said. When

Nicole's sister stared at her in disbelief, Dina continued, "Don't try to deny it. You've hated having to ask Nicole for every dime you spend. If she were out of the way, your obstacles would all be gone."

I nudged Grace, and when she looked at me, I shook my head slightly. We could supply something of value here, but I wanted to see what the others might say first.

To my surprise, it was Celia who spoke up first. "You don't know what you're talking about, Dina. We had that conversation on the drive up the mountain. Nicole is worried about my best interests, so she asked me to extend the conservatorship. I declined, and she accepted my answer. Everything is fine between us. Right, Sis?"

Nicole nodded. "I showed the paper to Celia, explained my reasoning, and she refuted every point I made. It was all very civil. In less than seven days, she gets the entire amount of the residual trust, and I couldn't be happier for her. After all, managing it has been one headache that I can do without." She paused as she looked pointedly at Janelle and Georgia. "Besides, we all know that I have enough to do as it is with my new job."

Janelle had the decency to look away, though Georgia continued to stare at her without flinching. If she'd been the one to fabricate that sales sheet, she was not being the least apologetic about it.

"Now who else? Anyone? Come now."

"I know it may look as though I wanted you out, but I never would have tried to kill you," Janelle said.

"Oh, and I would?" Georgia asked. "Seriously? You wanted that job just as badly as I did. I have to hand it to you, Janelle. I didn't think you had the brains to come up with that frame job."

"That's because I didn't," Janelle protested.

Georgia grinned at the statement. "Does that mean that you

didn't do it, or you weren't smart enough to think of it? Which is it, dear?"

"Let's not get off track," Nicole said, and then she stared at Dina before speaking again. "Would you care to share with the others what happened between us?"

Dina at least had the good sense to look flustered. "I keep telling you, it was all just one big misunderstanding. I thought you said high risk, not low risk, when you invested that money with me. I'm sorry you lost most of your life savings, but it wasn't my fault. I can't be held responsible for what the market does."

Nicole wasn't buying her explanation, and I felt that this was a good time to bring out more ammunition. "Is that why you packed a waiver of liability with you?" I asked Dina.

"Have you been snooping through my things?" she asked me harshly.

Nicole smiled for one brief moment. Now she knew what we'd been up to when she'd caught us earlier. At least part of it, at any rate. "Instead of deflecting your anger, maybe you should explain yourself."

"It was a standard form," Dina said. "It's not necessary at all."

"Then why bring it with you for Nicole to sign?" Grace asked her.

"My boss insisted that I do it," Dina explained. "You're not going to pin anything on me, so you might as well not try."

"What about the other paper we found in your case?" I asked her, smiling as sweetly as I could manage. "How are you going to explain that?"

Dina had been caught, and she knew it. "So what? Just because I practiced signing Nicole's name didn't mean that I was going to try to kill her." She turned to her now former best friend. "I thought you might be stuffy about not signing it, and my boss said that if I didn't bring it back with your signature on it, I'd be out of a job. I wasn't really going to forge your signature. It was just an emergency backup plan."

Nicole's lack of comment was chilling enough. No matter what else happened until we were finally rescued, I knew that particular friendship was dead, now and forever.

Almost as an afterthought, Dina added, "I don't know why you're so upset about it. It's not that big a deal."

"It is to me, and the fact that you feel that way speaks volumes about your character," Nicole said. She sighed heavily, and then she said, "All of this duplicity has made me tired of being around you all. I'm going for a walk, and don't any of you try to stop me."

I bounced up out of my seat. "I'm afraid I can't let you do that, Nicole."

"And why not?" she asked me icily.

"I don't mind you going out, but somebody's going with you. If you don't want Grace or me, I'm sure that someone else will be glad to accompany you, but like you said earlier, we're sticking together from here on out. Whoever tried to kill you before might not miss the mark the next time."

Nicole considered my words, frowned for a moment, and then she nodded. "Very well. I give up. You have all managed to beat me down to the point where I'm not even all that certain that I care about my personal safety anymore."

"It's going to be okay," Celia said as she moved toward her sister. "I'm here for you." She reached out and patted Nicole's hand, who smiled softly at the gesture.

"Thank you. I can't tell you how much I appreciate that."

"That's all well and good," Georgia said, "but we can't exactly stay in each other's hip pockets until help arrives. What are we supposed to do in the meantime?"

It was an excellent question.

I just wished that I had an answer for it.

CHAPTER 16

DINA WALKED OVER TO THE window and looked out. "Would you look at that? The snow is starting to melt."

"Great," Georgia replied. "We have three more hours of daylight, and then it's probably all going to start freezing again. We're never getting out of here, are we?"

"That's not why I said it," Dina replied as she grabbed the hooded sweatshirt she'd been issued along with the rest of us. "I don't care if anyone comes with me or not, but I'm going to see if Hank's body is still out there, so I don't have to sleep with one eye open all night."

"You can't go alone," Nicole commanded. "Regardless of how I feel about you, it's much too dangerous."

"Nobody's trying to kill me. Besides, would you really be all that upset if I joined Hank at the bottom of that gulley?" she asked her. "Nicole, I said that I was sorry. I don't know what else I can do."

"You can pay her back the money you lost out of your own funds," Celia said.

"If I could, don't you think that I would?" Dina asked, and then she left us without waiting for reinforcements.

I grabbed my own sweatshirt and started out after her.

"Where do you think you're going?" Georgia asked me.

"It's the buddy system, remember?"

"Wait for me," Grace said.

It was clear that Nicole wasn't happy about it, but she said, "That's it. We're all going."

"If you're coming, then you need to hurry up," I said. I couldn't wait around for them all to get their sweatshirts. Dina could be long gone by then.

I didn't hesitate as I took off after her.

The only problem was that she wasn't where I'd expected her to be. As I approached the spot where Hank had fallen over the side, there was no sign of Dina.

"Where did she go?" Grace asked me when she caught up with me.

"I have no idea," I said. The snow was no longer good for seeing footprints, or anything else, for that matter.

"Can you see if Hank is still down there?"

"I haven't had a chance to look yet." Why was I hesitating? Was it because I was afraid that he'd be there or that he wouldn't be?

Taking a deep breath, I peered over the side, half expecting to find Dina's body down there beside him, locked in some kind of deathly tableau.

Enough snow had melted so that I could see the spot where Hank had landed clearly now.

The only problem was that there was no body there anymore. There was something dark near the line of trees, but I couldn't say whether it was just a depression or an actual body hiding in the shadows.

Evidently Grace had been right.

The district manager might not have been killed instantly by the fall after all.

It appeared that he might be very much alive, and that led to all sorts of possibilities, none of them good for the rest of us.

"He's gone," Grace said after a moment looking over my shoulder.

"Why do you sound so surprised? You predicted it yourself this morning."

"Saying it and believing that it's true are two different things," she said. "That still doesn't explain where Dina is."

In my discovery of Hank's absence, I'd forgotten all about Dina. "She couldn't have just vanished."

"Why not? After all, Hank did," Grace reminded me.

If she saw the same dark area below that I did, she didn't mention it, so neither did I. "He didn't just disappear. Clearly we overestimated the impact of his fall. That still doesn't explain where Dina is, though."

The others soon joined us, and it was up to me to break the news to them. "Hank's body isn't down there anymore."

"I don't believe it," Nicole said as she peered down over the edge.

"We all saw him there! He was dead!" Janelle was in danger of losing it when Georgia grabbed her shoulders and gave her a hard shake.

"Snap out of it, Janelle! This is good news, remember?"

"To anyone but the person who shoved him," Grace said softly beside me.

"Janelle?" I asked her softly. "Is there something you want to tell us?"

The implication of my question finally hit her. "What? Do you think I did it? There's no way I'd shove him like that."

"I was the original target, though, remember?" Nicole reminded her. "You had a beef with me, didn't you?"

"Maybe so, but not enough to kill you," she said.

"So you say," Georgia answered, neatly pivoting back to the antagonist's role yet again.

"Would you make up your mind?" Celia protested. "Either you're this woman's friend or you're not. You're driving us crazy with your flip-flopping. I'm just glad that Hank is still alive."

She may have been the one to say it, but I was pretty sure that the rest of us had been thinking it.

"I don't know what you're talking about," Georgia said.

"Enough," I interjected. "We have two missing members of our party now, and it's going to be getting dark in a few hours, so we need to find both of them."

"How do you propose we go about doing that?" Nicole asked. She seemed fairly calm, given the circumstances.

"Half of us need to look for Hank outside, and the other half need to look for Dina. We don't have a great deal of time, so we're going to need to split up into two groups after all," I said. "Grace, why don't you and Celia come with me, and we'll look for any sign that Hank climbed back up that hill, either here or somewhere else. Nicole, you take Georgia and Janelle and see if you can find Dina."

It was fairly clear that Nicole wasn't interested in the team I'd assigned her, but let her deal with her problem employees. I was done with their bickering, and I wasn't all that certain that either one of them, alone, would be much better. Georgia took verbal shots at every opportunity, while Janelle's martyr complex was getting on my nerves just as much. I hadn't been all that certain about Celia at first, but after spending some time with her away from her sister, I was starting to warm up to her.

Nicole wasn't having any of that, though. "My sister stays with me. You can have either one of mine, but I get Celia."

"It's okay," Celia said, trying to calm her sister down. "I want to go with Suzanne and Grace. Don't worry, I'm sure they'll look out for me."

"You bet we will," Grace said.

"I'm not so sure that I like being anyone's second choice," Georgia said, and I saw Janelle nod in agreement.

Before we wasted any more time debating, I said, "We'll all meet back at the lodge when we're finished. Be careful, everyone."

With that, I led my team away from the edge and toward the road. I planned on going as far as I could on foot with Grace and Celia until I satisfied myself that Hank hadn't come that way. Glancing over my shoulder, I saw Nicole's team heading for the boathouse, which was as good a plan as any. Maybe I should have taken the search for Dina for myself, but I thought tracking Hank down would be more complicated, and I'd had experience investigating before. Still, I hoped that Nicole would check the gazebo, the cottages, and even the maze. Dina could be anywhere.

For that matter, so could Hank.

"I still don't know how he could survive that fall," Celia said. "He's strong, but I didn't think he'd be that strong."

"How well do you know him?" I asked her as we tracked the land below us by intermittently peering over the edge. In a hundred feet, I noticed something that I'd missed before. There was a hiking path of some sort below us, close to the level where Hank had fallen. What had looked to be an arduous climb after the fall was soon a worn path. The real question, though, was where did it ultimately lead?

Celia replied, "We had dinner together a few times. With Nicole, of course," she said. Was that a glint in her eye when she spoke of him? Maybe little sister had a crush on big sister's onetime boyfriend. It wouldn't be the first time it had ever happened in the history of the world.

"What do you think about his relationship with your sister?" Grace asked her as we continued to walk toward the Shadow Mountain Resort entrance.

"They were never right for each other," she said.

"How about you?" I asked her gently.

"What are you talking about? Me and Hank? No. No way. Of course not. That's insane."

She was protesting an awful lot over a lightly made suggestion, which led me to believe that was exactly what was going on. Celia must have been crushed when she thought that he was dead.

"Sorry. I was just wondering."

"Well, you can put your mind at ease," she said. "Hank and I are just friends."

Was she actually blushing, or were her cheeks red from the cold? I couldn't say. We approached the sign at the entrance, and I noticed something that I'd missed before. There was another, smaller sign off to one side. TRAIL TO WIDOW'S FALLS. So the path actually led somewhere after all. I had started down it when Celia grabbed my arm. "Where are we going?"

"Isn't it obvious? We need to follow this path until we get to the spot where Hank fell."

"He's not there anymore, though," Celia protested. "I saw it with my own eyes."

"That doesn't mean that he's not still down there somewhere and in trouble," I said. Another thought had occurred to me when I'd first seen that Hank was gone. The fall might not have killed him, but it still could have injured him badly enough to eventually end his life. I beat myself up for not realizing how close he'd fallen to an actual path. If we'd gone down there when it happened, we might have been able to help him. Then again, the trail we were now on, if it could actually be called that, was dangerous enough in the slush, even in the broad light of day. Doing it at night would have probably caused one or more of us to fall as well. I still wished that I'd known about it. Even with the odds against us, I wouldn't have been able to rest until we'd at least tried. I hadn't been that big a fan of Hank's, but that didn't mean that I'd wanted him to die out there in the elements, cold, injured, and alone. I wouldn't wish that fate on my worst enemy.

We kept going on the path, keeping a lookout for any sign that Hank had passed that way, but there were no footprints to be seen, just layers of slush and mud beneath. Surely he would have made some kind of impact on the path if he'd come that way. By the time we got to the place where our trail veered away from the spot where Hank had fallen, I'd just about given up hope of finding him, dead or alive.

And then I spotted something fluttering in the breeze ahead of us.

Was it Hank or something else?

There was only one way to find out.

After I pointed it out to the others, we decided that we had no other choice but to press forward and see what it could be.

Unfortunately, we'd been right the first time, though not immediately.

Evidently, Hank had recovered enough from his fall to crawl a dozen feet away into the dense undergrowth beyond our line of sight from above, and it pained me to think of him as he tried to save his own life by inching his way along, only to die in the effort.

CHAPTER 17

"**O**H, NO," CELIA CRIED OUT the moment she spotted him. "I can't believe he's dead!" She threw herself onto the body before we could stop her, and her sobs tore through her as she mourned what might have been, at least in her mind.

I knelt down and put a hand on her shoulder. "Celia, I know you're in pain, but we need to take a step back and think through what this means."

"I know exactly what it means! It means that someone killed him!" she shouted as she turned on me.

I looked at Grace, and she came closer to us. In a calming voice, she said, "Celia, let's step out of the way for a minute. Suzanne needs to check out a few things."

"Like what?" she asked as she allowed Grace to help her up. "He's dead! He feels so cold. I wish we'd brought a blanket with us."

It didn't make any sense given the circumstances, but I understood it nonetheless. I knew that at times like she was facing, doing anything was better than doing nothing at all, even if the end result was the same. Once Grace had her off to one side, I studied Hank's body. His hands were bruised from his effort to crawl toward help, and there was blood on his left temple. He might have survived the fall, but the strike on his head had ultimately done him in. It hadn't been an intentional murder, at least not as far as I could tell, but he'd still been killed in an attempt on someone's life. If only he'd been able to give us a clue as to who had pushed him. I searched him as gently as I could, but I found nothing that might point to one of our suspects. If only he'd tried to leave us a message with his last throes of life instead of trying to save it, we might know exactly who he'd saved Nicole from.

I stood and brushed off my hands.

Grace asked me, "Anything?"

"No," I said, shaking my head.

"That's too bad," she answered.

Celia looked at us as though we were speaking Greek. "Suzanne, what were you looking for?"

"Any indication as to who might have pushed him," I admitted.

"What does it matter now?" she asked me. "He's going to be just as dead whether we find anything or not."

"Don't you want his killer caught?" Grace asked her. "The only thing we have left to give him is justice."

"You're right," she said, drying her eyes with the back of her sweatshirt arm. "But there's nothing there, is there?"

"Maybe he left something at the place he fell," Grace suggested.

"I'll go look," I volunteered.

"I'll come with you," Grace said, but Celia grabbed her arm and wouldn't let her go.

"Do you have to leave me with him?" she asked, nearly sobbing again.

"No, I'll stay with you," Grace said as she shrugged in my direction and mouthed the word "sorry."

It was up to me. I followed Hank's path from where he'd fallen. It wasn't as though it was a very hard trail to backtrack. He'd not only scraped the dirt on his way, but he'd also destroyed several small bushes and seedling trees, pulling himself along until he reached some kind of shelter. As I got closer to the spot where he'd landed, I searched the ground all around it. The slush left behind was translucent, and I could see if there'd been anything left behind.

As far as I could tell, there wasn't.

Hank had died in vain after all, without leaving us a single clue.

But there still might be a way to work his demise in our favor. It meant lying to the others, but it was the only chance we had.

"I've got an idea," I told them when I approached.

"Did you find anything?" Grace asked me.

"No."

"Then what good is having an idea?" Celia asked me harshly.

"It all hinges on you, as a matter of fact," I said, doing my best to pump up her ego. "If you can pull it off, we have a chance of catching the killer red-handed." I knew that playing to her ego was a way of getting her to cooperate, and I felt a little guilty about manipulating her when she was so vulnerable, but what choice did I have? Jake liked to watch poker on television sometimes in the evening to relax after I went to bed, and I'd stayed up and watched enough of it to realize something. Sometimes, even when you don't have very good cards, you can still bluff your way to a win.

And that was exactly what I was about to propose.

"What do you say, Celia? Are you up for it?"

"I'll do whatever you ask me to," she said.

"Are you willing to lie to everyone else, even to your own sister?" I asked as the most important follow-up question that I could.

"I don't want to do that," she said, pouting a little.

"What if it were for her own good?"

Celia seemed to think about that, and then she finally nodded in agreement. "If it might help keep her safe, then I'll do it. Tell me what you have in mind."

"Yes, I'd like to know that as well," Grace said.

"As far as the rest of the party is concerned, Hank is still alive. Not only that, but we're going to tell them that we saw clear evidence that he is somewhere on the grounds and intent on exacting revenge."

They were both caught off guard by my suggestion, but Grace instantly smiled as she nodded slightly in agreement. "It's brilliant, if we can pull it off."

"I don't understand," Celia said. "How does this help us find out who killed him?"

"If they think Hank is still alive and that he poses a threat to whoever pushed him, someone might get careless enough to make a mistake. All we need is a thin wedge to split this wide open. If we tell everyone the truth about what we found, we've managed to lose one of the few advantages we have—the element of surprise." I looked at Celia, who was now nodding, albeit reluctantly. "What do you say? We can't do it without you."

"My first reaction is to say no, but the more I think about it, it's the last thing I can do for Hank, so even if it means lying to my sister, I'm on board."

"It's agreed, then," I said. "We tell them we saw evidence, maybe footprints, that made their way along the trail we just covered, and maybe we even found something of Hank's that couldn't have been there otherwise."

I looked at Celia, who was studying the body. "Hey, are you okay? If you don't want to do this, we don't have to. Maybe we can come up with something else."

She took a deep breath and then let it out before she spoke. "No, you're right. Neither one of you knew Hank very well, but he always carried a red bandana with him. It was a way to remind him of his late grandfather, and I found it endearing. If we take his bandana and plant it somewhere to show that he was there, we can 'prove' that he never died. The only question is who is going to retrieve it."

"I'll do it," I said, moving over to Hank's body before I had a chance to change my mind.

Only it wasn't there.

I patted his pockets down twice, and then Celia frowned. "I'm an idiot."

"Why? Wasn't he carrying one after all?" I asked her.

"It's what caught our attention in the first place," she said as she moved to the tree where we'd seen something flapping in the breeze when we'd first arrived.

Hank had used his bandana as a signal, the very thing that had led us to his body, and the item we were going to use to shake up his real killer.

I collected the small cloth square, and then I asked her, "Was there anything else Hank was known for?"

"Won't the bandana do? I thought it was perfect," Celia said with a frown.

"It is. As a matter of fact, it's too good to waste just yet. We need something else to show that he made it out of this in one piece."

Celia frowned, and finally, it was Grace who spoke next. "How about his button?"

"That's perfect," Celia said.

"Button? What button? How can that do us any good?"

Grace walked hesitantly to the body, and then she reached down and unpinned a button he'd been wearing on his sweatshirt. I'd missed it completely on my quick inventory earlier, but I didn't beat myself up about it. After all, I'd wanted to make the search as quick as possible.

It was a circular button the size of a quarter, and inside, it had the letters printed, TUIT.

"I don't understand," I said as I frowned at the button.

"Hank used to say that was most people's downfall. They always said they'd do something, but they never made time to actually accomplish their tasks."

Grace shrugged. "It's understandable that you don't see it, Suzanne. I had to ask him about it myself on the first day we met. It's a round tuit. Around to it. He told me that he always knew that someday he'd get a round tuit, and he always laughed every time he told the joke. I'm willing to bet there's not another one of these within a hundred miles. Everyone will know that it was his."

"Good enough," I said. "We're going to take this back as proof that he's still alive. There's just one thing left to do. Where do we say we found it?"

"How about on the front steps of the main lodge?" Celia suggested.

"I don't know how we'd explain the fact that no one else saw it there first," I explained. "It has to be in plain sight, but not in easy reach."

I was still considering possibilities when Celia countered, "We could say we found it on the sign for the resort."

"So, our story would be that he didn't lose it by accident but that he planted it so someone could find it," I said.

"What's wrong? Is that no good?" Celia asked.

"On the contrary. I think it's perfect. Grace, do you have an opinion?"

"I like it, too," she said. "It could be read as a warning to the killer, that Hank is going to get around to unmasking them, and soon."

"Only he can't," Celia said, getting a little weepy again.

"That's why we're going to do it for him," I said. "Now let's get going. It's going to be getting dark soon, and I don't know about the rest of you, but I don't want to be on this path when night falls."

"Lead the way," Grace said, but Celia didn't make any move to follow us.

"Is something wrong?" I asked her gently as she stood over the body.

"We can't just leave him like this," she said. "I know we can't drag him back up the path we crossed, but this just doesn't feel right to me."

"I know, but what can we do?" I asked her. "There's no way to protect him now." And no need, I added to myself silently.

"Shouldn't we at least say something over him?" she asked.

Grace saved the day. She looked at me, nodded solemnly, and then she took each of our hands in hers. As we stood there, she said, "Hank, you may be gone, but you will be missed. You may have sacrificed yourself to save someone else, but it won't be in vain. You may leave nothing but a memory behind, but it will be a good one, a last act of courage trying to protect someone else." She stopped, and we stood there a few moments before she spoke again, this time directly to Celia. "Is that what you had in mind?"

"It was beautiful," Celia said. "Thank you."

I mouthed the same sentiment to Grace myself. She'd done beautifully, but I would have expected nothing less from her. My best friend had a way with words, while I had a way with dough. Both assets were valuable, but at that moment, I would have traded every donut I'd ever made in my life for the ability to say something so powerfully.

CHAPTER 18

WE FOUND THE OTHER GROUP standing in front of the gazebo. "Did you have any luck?" Nicole asked us as we approached them.

"Hank wasn't where we saw him yesterday," I said as I shrugged. It was even true, since Hank had managed to crawl a little before he'd died.

Nicole looked perplexed. "Then why doesn't he show himself?"

"I don't know, but we found this," Grace said as she approached the others. "It was stuck to the sign for the resort." She handed the TUIT button to Nicole, who passed it to Georgia.

Janelle took it in turn, studied it, and then started to hand it back to Nicole. "I still don't get why he valued this thing so much."

"Hank loved wordplay and puzzles, basically anything that took a little creativity and cleverness to get," Celia said as she stepped up and took it before Nicole could. "He cherished this. He'd have sooner gone out without wearing pants than this button. The fact that we found it says volumes. I just wish I knew why he was hiding."

"It's pretty clear, isn't it?" Georgia asked.

"Not to me it isn't," Celia said. "Explain it."

"Hank is the only one of us who knows who tried to push Nicole off that cliff. I've got a hunch he's waiting for the right time to spring, and then whoever did it had better watch out.

After what he must have been through, he's not going to be very happy with the person who pushed him."

"His fall was an accident," Nicole said. "He was trying to save me, remember?"

"Do you think he still won't be upset just because he wasn't the original intended victim?" Georgia asked her.

"I take it you didn't have any luck finding Dina," I said, doing my best to change the subject.

"It's a mystery. She's vanished," Janelle said.

"I keep telling you, that's impossible," Georgia answered testily.

"Then where is she?" Janelle asked. "We've looked everywhere."

"Have you tried calling out her name?" I asked.

They all frowned, so I called out, "Dina! Dina! Where are you?"

"I'm in the maze," we all heard her say. "Is that you, Suzanne?"

"It is," I said as I glanced at the others. They hadn't even checked the maze in all the time that we'd been gone?

"We were going to look there next," Nicole said almost apologetically.

"But we got distracted by Georgia's constant complaining," Janelle replied.

"Hey, I can't be the only one who's cold and hungry," she answered.

"Are you okay?" I asked Dina loudly, ignoring the squabbling coworkers.

"I'm fine," she said. "Only I tried to get back out, and I'm afraid I'm a little lost."

"Don't worry. I'll be right there," I said as I headed for the maze.

"You're not going in there alone," Grace said.

"We can't all go," Georgia added. "Why don't you two go retrieve Dina, and the rest of us will go back to the lodge and see about dinner?"

"Are you actually offering to cook?" Janelle asked her. "We both know that you could burn water."

"I can do a little better than that, but I was thinking more along the lines of seeing what wouldn't need too much prep work. You're the mom of the group. Surely you can cook something edible for the rest of us."

"Just stay out of my way," Janelle said. I wasn't at all sure when she'd gotten so assertive, but it was working for her. Even Georgia seemed to be grudgingly respectful of her attitude.

Nicole hesitated before following the rest of them. "Celia, are you coming with us?"

"If you don't mind, I thought I'd go with Grace and Suzanne," she said softly.

"We don't have to stay with the same groups we were in before," Nicole replied.

"I know. I'm just not ready to deal with the two of them yet," she said as she pointed to Georgia and Janelle.

"At least you were spared some of it," Nicole said, adding a gentle smile. "I'll see you inside."

"Okay," Celia answered, and then she turned to us. "Do we need to look at the map again?"

I tapped my forehead. "That won't be necessary. It's all up here."

"Then we're in serious trouble," Grace said with a grin. "You know, you really could have gone back with your sister, Celia."

"I can see her any time," she said. "Besides, you two are a lot more fun to be around at the moment than she is."

"I won't argue with that, but then again, no one tried to kill either one of us," I said as I started toward the maze. "Dina, how about talking loudly so we can get a fix on exactly where you are?"

From inside the maze, she asked, "What should I talk about?"

"Anything will do. What interests you?"

118

"I could talk about investing," she volunteered.

It might put me to sleep before I found her, but if it was truly what she knew best, who was I to stop her? "Okay, that's fine. I have to warn you, though. Your advice will be falling on deaf ears as far as I'm concerned. I keep my life savings in a coffee can under my bed. I'd put it somewhere safer, but I can't imagine anyone being interested in my three hundred eleven dollars, can you?"

"You'd be amazed by what that little bit could do for you, if you invested it wisely," she said. The woman had nerve, I had to give her that. She'd recently lost what must have been a great deal of Nicole's money in the stock market, and here she was trying to give us financial advice. I had a hunch that my money was safer right where it was. Sure, it wouldn't grow any, but it wouldn't vanish, either. As far as I was concerned, that was a victory.

"How would you go about it?" I asked her.

"Well, first we'd put you in the market. With that amount, I believe I'd go for more aggressive stocks in hopes of quick growth."

Grace shook her head as she looked at me, and then she asked aloud, "Doesn't the prospect of fast growth also mean that it's by definition high risk?"

"What's life without taking chances every now and then?" Dina asked. "Besides, it's not nearly as risky as you might think."

Tell that to Nicole, I felt like saying, but I didn't think that would do me any good with the investment counselor. I knew that many people swore by their investments, but the one time I'd bought a little stock, it had unfailingly dropped from the moment of my initial purchase until it was virtually worthless. All in all, I preferred to hold onto what little I had.

"Do you have any ideas about what I should do with my inheritance?" Celia asked her. "I'm about to come into a fairly healthy amount. No one thinks I can be prudent with it, so I'd love nothing more than to prove them all wrong."

You could almost hear Dina salivating at the news. "We need to talk, dear girl. I have a few things in mind for you, but trust me, I'm going to make you rich."

I touched Celia's shoulder, and then I shook my head, indicating that I thought it was a very poor idea to take financial advice from this woman.

Celia grinned at me, and then she said softly, "I'm not letting her anywhere near my money. I'm just trying to keep her talking so we can find her and get out of here. I'm getting cold, too," she added, shivering a little from the chill in the air. The sky was definitely beginning to darken, and I knew that before long, we'd never be able to get Dina out of there.

Her voice sounded closer, though.

"I've got an idea. Why don't you sing the alphabet song," I suggested. It really didn't matter what she said or even sang, but I was tired of her pitches, so I wanted an alternative to home in on.

"That sounds a bit silly to me," she said.

"Then I don't care what you sing. Just give us something to help us find you."

Surprising me with her choice, she began to sing an old-time hymn, one that I hadn't heard in years. To my amazement, Dina had a fairly decent voice. Using it to guide us, we soon found her.

"That was nice, Dina," Grace said. "You can really sing."

"Thanks. I used to sing in my grandmother's church choir when I was younger. I don't know what made me think of that song. I haven't sung it in years."

Grace looked at me, a little mortified. "Suzanne, I was so intent on finding Dina that I lost track of how we got in here. Are we lost, too?"

I grinned at her. "No worries. I kept track."

"How?"

"In my mind," I said with a smile.

"Then we're doomed. We're all doomed," she answered with a grin of her own.

I only led us down one false path before we made our way out of the maze. Considering the circumstances, I thought that was pretty good.

Once we were all free of the maze, we headed back to the lodge. There still weren't any electric lights on in the massive stone building, but I could see flickering lights and shadows being thrown off from the fireplace within. No one would go cold tonight, and based on what I'd seen in the pantry on my previous raids, no one should go hungry, either. I fingered the bandana in my pocket, still safely tucked away. I wasn't sure how I would use it, but I knew that having it might come in handy, so I wasn't about to reveal its presence without coming up with a very good way to scare the killer into making a mistake.

"Did you ever find Hank?" Dina asked me, pulling me from my thoughts.

"When we got there, he was gone," I said. That was true as well, since in my world, being gone could mean that someone just left or that they'd died, taking a rather more serious leave of the rest of us.

"That is so weird," Dina said. "I'm not happy with this game of hide-and-seek he's playing with us."

"I'm still not sure that it involves all of us," Celia said, speaking up for the first time in a while.

"What do you mean?"

"I have a hunch that he's just interested in the person who tried to kill him last night, don't you think?"

"You've probably got a point, but then again, I've never had that kind of experience before myself, so it's hard to say."

I found it difficult to believe that no one had threatened Dina before, especially given the fact that it was highly likely that Nicole hadn't been the only client she'd bankrupted. "You're lucky, then. I've even had people come after *me* in the past."

For some reason, Dina found that amusing. "What could you have possibly done to someone to make them angry enough to want to kill you?"

I answered her with dead sincerity. "The truth of the matter is that I've backed more than one murderer into a corner in the past, and let me assure you, there's no more dangerous man or beast."

"But you make donuts for a living, right?" Dina asked me skeptically.

"And great ones at that," Grace said, rising to my defense. "But what she's really known for are her amateur sleuthing skills."

"I suppose that makes you her sidekick," Dina said disparagingly.

"Grace is my partner," I said proudly. "She's not anybody's sidekick. I wouldn't have been able to do most of what I've accomplished if it hadn't been for her."

"Thank you," Grace told me.

"You're most welcome. It's true, you know."

"I hate to interrupt your mutual admiration society," Dina said, "but I'm cold and hungry. Let's go in, shall we?"

"I just have one question before we rejoin the others," I said as I placed a hand lightly on her shoulder, keeping her from going in.

"What's that?"

"Why did you really run away earlier?"

Dina stopped, turned, and gave me a critical glance. "I told you when I left. I went to see if Hank was still there."

"But we never saw you on our search," Celia interrupted, getting into the swing of the investigation. "If that were true, we should have bumped into you somewhere on the trail below."

"I glanced over the hill, but I couldn't see him, and unlike you three, I must have missed the other trail. I didn't want to go back inside, though, not the way everyone else was acting, so I decided that what I really needed was a little time alone."

"So that's why you got lost in the maze?" I asked her.

"I didn't do it intentionally," Dina protested. "I probably should have studied the map before I went in, but I thought, how hard could it be? After all, I'd done it once before."

"These things aren't always easier the second time you go through them," I said.

"No kidding. Is that all, or do you have more questions for me?"

It was a legitimate inquiry, but I wasn't sure how to ask the most pressing question in my mind.

Once again, Grace took care of that for me.

"If you wouldn't mind sharing with the rest of us, were you the one who tried to push Nicole over the edge of the cliff?"

"Don't be ridiculous," she snapped.

I didn't let go of her shoulder, though. "That's not really an answer, is it?"

"I don't have to reply to such insane questions," Dina said as she broke free of my grip.

"Maybe not," Celia said, "but if you didn't do it, you should be more than happy about freely admitting your lack of involvement in what happened."

"Is that what you all want from me, a declaration of my innocence?" she asked, nearly at the point of tears. I hadn't realized how stressed she was until I could see the hopelessness in her gaze. "Fine. I didn't try to push Nicole over the edge, nor did I shove Hank by mistake. There, are you satisfied?"

"Until new information comes to light, it will do," Grace said.

"Don't hold your breath, because it's not going to, at least not as far as I'm concerned. Now, if you all will excuse me, I'm going to warm myself up by the fire and wait for dinner."

Before we three followed Dina inside, I turned to Grace and Celia. "What do you think? Was she telling the truth, or was she lying to us?"

"I wish I knew," Celia said. "The problem is that she probably lies to people all the time about their investments. It's like anything else. If she's gotten enough practice, she's bound to be good at it by now."

I nodded, and then I turned to Grace, who said, "Celia makes a good point. Honestly, I just don't know."

"Then we keep our eyes and ears open until we can learn more," I said.

"Are you two trying to solve Hank's murder?" Celia asked us both hopefully.

I didn't have the heart to tell her that we were working on something else entirely, but then again, maybe we weren't. Hank's murder and the attempt on Nicole's life were two pieces of the same puzzle. Discovering one identity should lead us directly to the other. "We are," I said.

Grace raised an eyebrow at my statement, but she nodded all the same.

Celia seemed satisfied with our responses. "If there's anything I can do, all you have to do is ask, and if it's within my power to grant, I will."

"Thank you," I told her, and the three of us walked into the lodge, hopefully ready for whatever the rest of the night had in store for us.

CHAPTER 19

"WHAT ARE YOU MAKING US for dinner?" Georgia asked me as I walked into the lodge.

"When did I become the designated chef around here?" I asked. "I thought Janelle was cooking tonight."

"You're the only professional cook around here. Do you really trust her abilities in the kitchen? Why *wouldn't* you feed us?" Dina asked.

"I make donuts for a living. If you want them again, I'm your gal, but someone else needs to prepare a meal tonight."

"I said earlier that I'd be happy to make something," Janelle insisted.

"We don't want anything you'd make for your kids," Georgia complained.

"I for one am willing to eat whatever you feel like making, Janelle," I said.

Grace nodded as well. "Go on, dazzle us, Janelle."

She looked uncomfortable with the sudden attention. "I wasn't planning on making anything all that special. Let me see what I can come up with."

I was starting to feel guilty about not agreeing to cook, so I followed her into the kitchen. "Janelle, I can help out, if you'd like."

She smiled softly at me. "No, I don't mind. Really. It might help take my mind off what's been going on here this weekend."

Jessica Beck

"It's been pretty spectacularly bad, hasn't it?" I asked her sympathetically.

"I just can't believe that Hank is hiding out somewhere, waiting to pounce on one of us. He's never been what you'd call a great guy, but I can't imagine him lurking in the shadows watching us. I have to admit, I never pegged him as the hero type when he tried to save Nicole. Lying in wait is more his style, but it still gives me the creeps knowing that he's out there somewhere. Or even in here."

I saw Janelle shiver at the thought of her former boss skulking in the shadows, and I knew that I could offer her a bit of comfort by telling her that Hank wouldn't be able to do anything to anyone ever again, but we'd come up with our plan of keeping him alive in everyone else's minds for a reason, and it was still valid as far as I was concerned. No, at least for the moment, I had to play along. "It didn't hurt that he was trying to save someone he once loved," I said.

"I'm not sure that what he and Nicole ever had could have been called love," Janelle said, again surprising me with her candor. Put her in a crowd of other people and she was mostly quiet unless she felt compelled to defend herself, but get her alone, and she was actually quite chatty.

"Do tell," I said as I took one of the stools and pulled it over near the workspace.

"Give me one second," she said.

Janelle disappeared into the large pantry, and when she came back out, her hands were full. After she put everything down on the counter, she reached for a large pot and filled it from the tap. Once she was happy with the level of water, she set it on the largest burner and turned it to high. Taking another, smaller pot out, she put it on one of the supplemental burners and emptied two large cans of tomato sauce into it.

"Are we having spaghetti?" I asked her.

"What's wrong? Don't you like it?"

"I adore it," I said. "Your sauce might need a little something, though." I could just imagine the howls if she tried serving noodles and tomato sauce to that crowd.

"Oh, don't worry. I'm just getting started." Janelle grabbed a few green bell peppers she'd brought along, as well as a pair of onions and some carrots.

"Carrots?" I asked her.

"I do it with my kids all the time. It's a good way of getting your vegetables, and they add a nice texture to the sauce."

I wasn't about to disagree with her. After everything was peeled, chopped or diced, she added it to the sauce. Now it was time for her to doctor it with spices, and I was pleased to see that oregano was first on her list. I was about to suggest a dash or two of sugar to offset the acidity of the tomatoes when she did it on her own. Janelle appeared to be a pretty decent cook after all.

With the sauce simmering and while we waited for the pasta water to come to a full boil, I reminded her, "You were saying earlier?"

"What were we talking about again?" she asked.

"Nicole and Hank's love affair," I said.

Janelle frowned. "I shouldn't have said that."

"You're among friends here," I said. "It might help if I knew something about their relationship. Nicole broke up with him recently, is that right?"

Janelle glanced at the closed kitchen door before she'd answer. Lowering her voice anyway, she said, "Hank might have been infatuated with her, but I'm not so certain that Nicole returned those feelings. It always seemed to me that she endured his company, you know? Once she got the job she was after, she dropped him as though he were radioactive."

"How did he take it?"

"He was furious! That's why his final act of sacrificing himself surprised me so much." I could tell that there was something else on Janelle's mind, but she wasn't ready to share it with me yet. I wasn't sure how much time we had, though, as the pasta water started to boil. After she added a bit of sea salt and some olive oil to the water, in went enough pasta to feed an army. I knew we had somewhere around ten minutes before it would be ready, so I had to spur her on somehow.

"What can you tell me about that faked report?" I asked her.

"It was Georgia. It had to be, because I know that I didn't make it. She really wanted that job, Suzanne, more than I ever did. Sure, the extra money would have been nice, and I would have been okay with the title, but I didn't really want to be away from my kids more than I already am."

"But your rival doesn't have anyone at home, does she?"

Janelle shook her head. "She lives for her work, and if Nicole had actually been the one who'd gone over that cliff, I wouldn't have hesitated believing that Georgia had been the one to supply the shove."

"You didn't see anything actually happen, though, did you?"

"No, I missed it all," she said. "Still, if I were Nicole, I wouldn't turn my back on Georgia even now."

"Do you think she's still a threat, even after what happened to Hank?"

Janelle shrugged. "Think about it. She hasn't achieved her main goal yet, has she? We're out here isolated in the middle of nowhere, cut off from the outside world. If she's going to strike again, it has to be while we're all here."

"Do you really think she's that cold-blooded?"

"I do," Janelle said.

"What about the others?" I asked.

"Well, I'm pretty sure that Grace didn't do it," Janelle said earnestly.

"I'll vouch for her myself," I said.

"You two are really good friends, aren't you?"

"The best."

"I haven't had that for a very long time. When Bryson left me, I lost touch with everyone but my two kids. I suppose they're my best friends these days." She sighed heavily and then added, "When they grow up and move away, I'll be all alone."

Her sadness was a pervasive presence in the room, and I knew that I should try to comfort her, but how? I patted her shoulder and said, "There's always time to make new friends, Janelle."

"Is that an offer? Would you be my friend, Suzanne?"

What? Where had that come from? My life was pretty full as it was, but I didn't have the heart to reject her. "Sure. Why not?"

Janelle stunned me by hugging me, and then I realized that she was crying! Grace took that moment to come into the kitchen, but the second she saw what was going on, she ducked back out of the room.

"Hey, are you okay?" I asked Janelle as I finally managed to pull away.

"I'm sorry. I just get so emotional when I'm stressed out," she apologized, wiping away the tears.

"If we all didn't feel at least a little bit stressed right now, we'd have serious problems," I said.

"Thanks, Suzanne." Janelle turned her attention back to the pot, reached into the boiling water with a fork, and plucked out a few pieces of pasta. Chewing one, she said, "Another minute ought to do it. Do you mind setting the table?"

"It's the least I can do," I said with a grin.

"No, the least you could do is what everyone else is currently doing," Janelle said with a smile. "Having you here is a real comfort to me."

"What can I say? It's the buddy system at work," I said as I set each place.

"I like that. I haven't had a buddy in a long time. It's kind of nice."

"It is at that," I said.

Janelle found a colander and drained the pasta, then she put it back in the pot. Tasting her sauce with a spoon, she nodded and offered me a taste. I took it, and was surprised by how good it was. "That's really nice."

"I know, right?" she asked with a smile. "You might as well let them know it's time to eat."

I wasn't sure that I'd gotten everything there was to know from Janelle, but it appeared that my time with her alone had run out, at least for the moment.

There were no complaints about the food, but not many compliments either, and by the time we were finished, I made a point of congratulating the chef. "Janelle, that was delicious. You worked wonders."

"It was okay, but I wouldn't give it five stars," Georgia sniped.

"Then you can show us how it's done tomorrow night," I said with a wicked grin.

"Do you honestly think that we'll still be here?" Celia asked worriedly. "Surely we'll be rescued by then."

"We're not exactly stranded on a desert island," Dina said. "This place isn't all that bad if you have to be stranded somewhere."

"We may as well be on an island," Nicole said. "I'm with my sister. The sooner we get away from here, the better."

"I can't blame *you* for feeling that way," Georgia said.

"What do you mean by that?" There was shrillness in Nicole's voice that I hadn't heard before. Clearly the strain was getting to her as well.

Georgia was evidently taken aback by her reaction as well. "Sorry. I didn't mean anything by it."

Nicole wasn't going to let it go, though. "Why don't I believe you? You should just say what you're really thinking."

"I just meant that it's got to be hard on you, knowing that someone tried to kill you," she answered meekly.

"Not just someone," Grace said. "Someone here at this very moment."

It quieted us all, and in the silence, I decided that it might be time to heighten the edginess even a little more. "I wonder where Hank is right now."

Celia frowned at me, but the others reacted more subtly.

"Could he really be inside the lodge?" Dina asked. "I can't imagine how we could have missed him."

"Are you kidding? This place is huge," Georgia answered. "You could hide a cow in here and no one would be able to find it for days."

"I'm not sure if I'd go quite that far, unless he was a stuffed cow." Her mention of a cow had made me think of Emily Hargraves and her three childhood stuffed animals, Cow, Spots, and Moose. I'd give just about anything to be back in April Springs at that moment to see what silly handmade outfits they were wearing instead of trapped on the mountain with a murderer.

Georgia looked at me as though I'd lost my mind, but Grace smiled at the reference, and I knew that she'd gotten it, at least. "Still, if I'd been the one who'd tried to shove Nicole, I don't think I'd be able to sleep tonight."

"Well, I didn't do it, so I'll sleep just fine," Georgia replied.

"I know that I didn't do it, either," Janelle said, "but that still doesn't mean that I'll be able to sleep a wink. Should we set up guard duty tonight so someone can watch out for us?"

"That would be fine, except what if the guard we pick is the attempted murderer?" Dina asked.

"We could always do it in pairs," Celia offered.

"I think that's a wonderful idea," Nicole said. "Celia, would you be my watch partner?"

"Sure," she said a little uneasily. Had she wanted to pair with Grace or me instead, or was there something else to her reluctance? Then I realized that given the fact that her sister was the killer's original target, why wouldn't she hesitate about being paired with her? It was the only sane reaction anyone could have had.

"Grace and I will take a shift," I said before Janelle could try to claim me for her own.

She looked disappointed by my move but then quickly recovered. "I'll take Dina," Janelle offered.

I wasn't sure who was more surprised by that, Georgia or Dina.

"That just leaves me. I suppose I could take a shift by myself," she said.

I couldn't allow that, especially if she was the murderer. "You know what? I don't mind doing double duty. After all, I'm used to being awake all hours of the night. If you all don't mind, Georgia and I can take the shift at two, and then Grace can relieve her at four."

"That's not fair to you, Suzanne," Janelle said. "You can't be expected to stay awake most of the night and then make us breakfast the next day as well."

"I can make pancakes," Celia volunteered.

"Since when did you learn how to cook?" Nicole asked her.

"You don't know everything there is to know about me, Sis," she said with a grin.

"So I see," Nicole answered. "Then we have a plan. It's too early for bed, though. What should we do until then?"

"We could always search the lodge again," Grace suggested.

I wondered why she'd suggest that, but if that was her play, then I was going to back her up. "I think that's a great idea."

"Have you both lost your minds?" Georgia asked. "It's dark out, so there won't be any light coming in through the windows.

We don't have any electricity, and I don't know about the rest of you, but the batteries in my flashlight are starting to weaken. The worst thing we could do is break up and search this place again."

"That's not the *worst* thing I can think of," Janelle replied.

Georgia looked affronted by the comment. "Oh, yeah? Name one thing worse."

"We could search the grounds outside," she said.

Georgia shrugged. "You're right. I was wrong. That *is* worse."

Janelle grinned slightly as she put a hand behind one ear. "Excuse me. I'm not sure I heard what you just said."

"You were right. Don't act so surprised. It was bound to happen sooner or later."

"We could always play a board game," Dina offered, pointing to a stack of games in one of the bookcases. "Just not Clue."

"I'm not sure Monopoly would be any better," Nicole said.

"We could sit by the fire and tell ghost stories," Grace said with a grin. It was something that only she would have said aloud, let alone thought of in the first place.

"On second thought, Monopoly sounds great."

We played, though none of us were focused on the outcome, and I soon pushed my money and properties into the center of the board. "If I'm going to pull two shifts, I need to get a little sleep."

I nodded to Georgia. "Wake me when it's our turn."

"Me? Your internal alarm clock has to be better than anything I can buy. If you're counting on me to wake you up, we'll both be sleeping until dawn."

"Don't worry. Dina and I will wake you when it's your turn," Janelle said.

I nodded and took one of the free couches far away from the game but closer to the fire. I'd chosen to serve with Georgia first. That way, while everyone else was asleep later, Grace and I could plant Hank's bandana somewhere and come up with some other way of frightening the killer into making a mistake. Out of consideration, they all lowered their voices after I curled up to sleep, but it still seemed to take me forever.

I must have managed to doze off at some point, though, because the next thing I knew, someone was shaking my shoulder. Had I honestly slept all that long, despite the fact that there was a killer among us, or had something gone wrong, and was I about to hear some very bad news indeed?

CHAPTER 20

"WHAT'S WRONG, CELIA?" I ASKED as I sat up and rubbed my eyes. "How long have I been asleep, anyway?"

"I'm sorry I woke you, but I didn't know what else to do. Nicole's missing!"

"What? Weren't you together?" I asked as I stood up and stretched. "I thought you were working as a team."

"I had to go to the bathroom," she admitted. "I was only gone two minutes, but when I came back in, she was gone. Suzanne, I'm worried about her."

It was clear that Celia was near her breaking point. "Take a deep breath and try to calm down. Don't worry, we'll find her."

"What if something happened to her because I couldn't hold it?"

"There's no reason to believe that anything's wrong," I said. "Where could she have gone?"

"That's what I've been trying to figure out," Celia said when I saw something dark coming down the stairs from the second floor. I grabbed an ancient golf club on display and got ready to defend both of us, but I didn't need it.

"What's up?" Nicole asked as she came into the firelight.

Celia ran to her and hugged her tightly. "I thought you were dead!"

"Why would you think that?" Nicole asked her. "I thought

I heard someone moving around upstairs, so I decided to check it out by myself."

"Why didn't you wait for me?" Celia asked her.

"I didn't want anything happening to you if I was right," Nicole confessed.

Maybe they weren't the best team to pair up after all. If the buddy system was going to work, that meant that everyone had to stay with their partners and not take any foolish risks on their own. I wasn't about to chide Grace's boss about it, though. Her heart had been in the right place, but I still needed to say something. "Nicole, you can't just wander off by yourself. If anyone needs a buddy watching their back, it's you."

She looked contrite. "You're right, Suzanne. It was foolish of me to take a risk like that. I'm sorry."

I hadn't been expecting an outright apology. "Just stay together while you're on duty, okay?"

"Okay," she promised. "Why are you awake, anyway?"

"That's my fault," Celia said. "When I couldn't find you, I panicked and woke her up."

"I'm doubly sorry now," Nicole said. "Suzanne, why don't you go back to sleep? We'll be fine from here on out, I promise."

"Okay, if you're sure," I said.

"Thanks," Celia said to me, and I nodded as I did my best to smile.

Settling back onto the couch, I tried to get back to sleep, but I soon realized that it was impossible. Getting back up, I approached the two sisters as they stood by the fire.

"Suzanne, you really need to at least try to sleep," Nicole scolded me.

"I did, but for now, I'll keep you two company."

"There's nothing to see here," Nicole said. "Really, I must insist."

"Nicole, she's a grown woman," Celia told her sister. "Let her do what she wants."

"You're right. I'm sorry. I'm just not myself this weekend."

"Who can blame you, Sis? Someone tried to shove you off a cliff! It would be enough to shake anybody up, and the thought that Hank is wandering around somewhere, probably in this lodge, makes it amazing to me that *anyone* can sleep. You must be distraught by what's been happening."

"I am, but I'll get through it, with your help."

We talked about a dozen different things, from running a donut shop to supervising a region of a large cosmetics company to making crafts and selling them online, which happened to be our three specialties. Soon enough, it was time for the next shift, and as Dina and Janelle took over, I decided to try one more time to sleep.

I finally managed to do it, but it seemed as though it were an instant later when someone was shaking my shoulder again. It was Georgia this time, and my night's rest was officially over. I'd been known to go into the donut shop and work on a depressingly small amount of sleep at times in the past, but this was going to be a challenge, even for me.

"I'm awake," I said as I stood and stretched. "Man, I'd kill for some coffee right about now."

"You're in luck," Georgia said, "because Dina made some just before she woke me."

"Did she not stay with Janelle?" Was nobody willing to follow the simplest rule, that you always stay with your partner?

"I don't know the details. Do you want some or not?"

It was too late to worry about it now, and I desperately needed something to wake me up. "I do," I said. "How can we get some and still watch the group?"

"Tell you what. You stand in the doorway between the reception area and the restaurant, and I'll prop the kitchen door open and fetch us both coffee. If either one of us sees anything out of the ordinary, help is just a shout away."

It wasn't ideal, but it would have to do. "Fine, but don't dawdle."

"No worries there. I'm no more eager to be alone here than you are."

Georgia came back quickly with two mugs, both emblazoned with the Shadow Mountain Lodge logo on them. I'd thought about buying one as a souvenir when we'd first arrived, but now I just wanted to wipe every memory of this place from my mind if we got away.

The coffee was stronger than I normally liked, but I drank it anyway.

Georgia and I stood in the dim light of the fire where we could watch everyone else as they slept as well as see the fire. Someone must have recently put fresh wood on it, because it was blazing nicely. If we hadn't had that fireplace, we'd all be huddled together somewhere trying to conserve every last bit of heat, but as it was, I saw that most of the women had not only thrown off their covers, but they'd taken off their hoodie sweatshirts as well. Only Nicole still wore hers, but in her defense, she was farthest from the fire.

"What do we do, just stand here for two hours and watch the flames?" Georgia asked me.

"We could always talk, as long as we keep our voices down," I suggested.

"Sure. Why not? What do you want to talk about?"

"How about that forged sales report?" I suggested.

Georgia glanced at me warily. "I was thinking more along the lines of the latest gossip in the entertainment world."

"As far as I'm concerned, discussing the events of this weekend is all I want to do at the moment. Did you do it, Georgia?"

"Why should I tell you anything, Suzanne?" she asked.

"I'm not in any position to hurt you with the information," I said.

"Why don't I believe you? If I say one word to you, you'll tell Grace or Nicole, and I'm sunk either way. Thanks, but no thanks."

I took a deep breath, and then I made a decision. "What if I promise that I'll keep whatever you tell me in confidence?"

"Even from Grace?" she asked me.

"Yes, even from her," I vowed.

"Suzanne, why should I believe you? I know what good friends you two are."

"Georgia, I wouldn't promise it if I weren't willing to abide by it. Do I want to share everything with my best friend? Of course I do, but if it means getting you to tell me something confidentially, I'm willing to make that sacrifice. Besides, wouldn't it feel good getting it off your chest?"

She frowned, and then, nearly shocking me by its unexpected nature, Georgia started to softly cry.

"Are you okay?" I asked her.

Georgia stopped crying and swiped her cheeks with her free hand. "I don't know what's gotten into me. All of a sudden I'm some kind of basket case."

"The stress we're all under would break a Navy Seal down," I said. "So tell me, just between the two of us, did you fake that report?"

She nodded, but then she quickly explained, "Just because it was faked didn't mean that it wasn't true."

"I don't understand," I said.

"Suzanne, what I'm about to tell you could get me fired. You can't tell anyone, but I've been thinking. If something were to happen to me, no one would know the truth. I have to trust someone with what I know. Can I trust you?"

"You can," I said. What kind of bombshell was she about to lay on me?

"I found a way to tap into the real-time sales records of all of the associates at our company. Don't ask me how, because I really don't know. I happened to stumble across the access code one day, and I've been using the information to my advantage ever since."

It wasn't stellar behavior, but I didn't think that it was criminal, either. "What did you see?"

"Nicole cheated just like Janelle and I did! That form might not have been the original, but the numbers it reflected were on the money. The only problem was that Nicole must have found some way to alter her numbers before Hank saw it. It made her sales look legit, while Janelle's and mine were suddenly tainted."

"Are you saying that neither one of you tried to game the system?" I asked her.

Georgia shook her head. "Of course we did. It was the way it was set up. What I'm saying is that Nicole did the same thing we did. She was just too smart to get caught doing it."

I didn't know if Georgia was lying to me or not. Could I believe her? Had Nicole really cheated, or was this just Georgia's way of justifying trying to sabotage her boss's promotion? "What were you going to do with the report?" I asked her.

"What do you think? I told Hank the moment we got here, and I even showed it to him."

"What was his reaction?" I decided that my best bet was to at least pretend to believe her for the moment. It was the only way I could get more information out of her. If I seemed skeptical in the slightest, then Georgia would shut up about it forever.

"He was furious," Georgia said. "He told me that he'd been looking for a reason to fire her since she broke up with him, and that report was all the ammunition he needed."

"Was he going to fire her while we were all here at the lodge?" I asked her.

"He asked me to keep the report until he needed it. Hank didn't trust anyone, and that included Nicole."

"And yet he risked dying trying to save her. That part doesn't make sense," I said.

"Who knows? Maybe he had a change of heart at the last second. After all, he said that he loved her. Maybe seeing her in danger made him momentarily forget what had happened. It could have just been instinct that made him save her."

"So you didn't push him off that precipice yourself?" I asked her calmly.

Georgia's voice got a little loud, but I didn't care if she woke anyone up at that point. "Why would I do that? He was going to fire her! I don't like Nicole, and everyone knows that I want her job, but I wouldn't kill her, and I certainly wouldn't have tried to get rid of the one man who could give me what I wanted."

"Calm down," I said. "I had to ask. So, if you didn't do it, who did?"

"My money's still on Janelle," she said.

"Seriously? I have a hard time seeing her do something like that."

"That's why it's so brilliant! It's so out of character for her that no one would suspect her, but I know something that no one else here knows. Her daughter needs surgery, and our insurance will only cover part of it. Janelle needs that bump in pay more desperately than anyone else knows. If it were just about her, I agree with you. She would never even consider it. But if it meant saving her daughter's life, I firmly believe that she'd kill every last one of us without a second thought."

I knew how strong a mother's love for her child could be, and Janelle certainly seemed truly devoted to her kids. Could Georgia be right? I'd have to rethink several things I'd been considering.

Either Georgia was telling the truth about everything, she was blatantly lying about it all, or there was a blend of honesty and deception that I wasn't clever enough to discern. Was it possible that Nicole had altered the numbers to make herself look better than her closest competitors? From what I knew of her, I supposed that it was. After all, she made no bones about buying the finest things she could afford, as evidenced by her wardrobe, so I was certain that she'd use every dime of the raise she'd gotten on more elegant clothing and jewelry. But I couldn't see her as a killer. Then again, no one fit my idea of a cold-blooded murderer. We were a group of saleswomen, a crafter, an investment manager, and a donutmaker. None of those descriptions fit the anatomy of a killer. Then again, I'd come to believe that given the right motivation, coupled with the exact amount of applied pressure and given the opportunity, just about anyone could turn into a murderer.

My head was spinning with possibilities, and I was faced with the prospect that I was no closer to unmasking the real murderer than I had been the moment we'd discovered Hank's body lying at the bottom of that ravine.

The real question was how could I go about winnowing the chaff of lies, deception, and misdirection, and finding the kernels of truth hidden somewhere within?

CHAPTER 21

"**G**RACE, IT'S TIME TO GET up," I said, happy for once to be shaking someone else's shoulder for a change.

She slapped my hand away instinctively. "Two more minutes, Mom."

"I'm not your mother," I said, laughing despite the situation. "Get up."

"Suzanne? What time is it?" Grace was really not a morning person, but to be fair, I'd already been up for hours. My schedule wasn't much different than if I'd been home in April Springs working at Donut Hearts, while I was positive the only way Grace would be awake so early was if she hadn't gone to sleep at all the night before.

"Here. Drink this." Georgia and I had made a fresh pot of coffee just before she'd gone to bed, so I was ready for Grace.

She took the mug in both hands after she sat up and drank deeply. "Okay, that's better. How do you do it, Suzanne?"

"Do what?"

"Get up so early every day."

"It's a real achievement," I answered. "Come on. I've got an idea."

"That sounds intriguing," she said as she stood, nearly spilling her coffee as she did so. Once we were away from the others, she asked, "What are we going to do?"

"Do you have any lipstick with you?" I asked her.

"Seriously? You want a makeover?"

"Don't be ridiculous. Do you have some, or don't you?"

"Sure," she said. "Let me get it out of my bag."

"Be quiet doing it," I reminded her. "We don't want to wake anyone up."

"You know me. I'm as quiet as a cat." She then proceeded to bang her big toe on an end table and nearly sent a lamp crashing to the floor before she managed to catch it at the last second, grimacing the entire time.

"Are you okay, kitty?" I asked her.

"I'll live. We both know that I'm not exactly at my best this time of day."

"You'll be fine."

She got her lipstick and handed it to me when she returned. "What are you going to use it for?"

"We're going to leave the killer a message," I said. "Follow me."

"What do you think?" I asked Grace as I stepped back and admired my work. I'd taken her lipstick and written a message on the hall mirror where someone was bound to see it sooner or later. It was far enough out of sight of the main reception hall not to be immediately noticeable, but once anyone approached it, they wouldn't be able to miss it.

In lipstick, I'd written,

"YOU'RE GOING TO PAY FOR WHAT YOU'VE DONE."

"Should you write something a little less vague?" she asked me.

"I would if I could, but in the first place, there's not a whole lot of room for a manifesto, and in the second, I can't be more specific than that, because I'm not exactly sure who it is that I'm threatening. I think it looks particularly ominous written in that shade of red, don't you?"

"It's ghastly," Grace agreed.

"There's just one last touch we need to add, and then we're both going to forget that it's even here."

"What are you going to do, stick a knife into the wall beside it?" Grace asked me.

"I hadn't thought of that. Do you think it would work?"

"It would certainly terrify me," she said. "Hang on. I'll be right back."

"I'm coming with you," I said as I started to follow her.

"You can't. What if somebody wakes up and sees this before we're ready? You need to stand guard and distract them. I'll just be two seconds."

"If I count to three and you're not here, I'm coming after you," I said.

"That's fine with me," Grace answered.

I knew that she was gone less then fourteen seconds, because I counted every last one of them, but it felt as though she'd left me an hour ago. I was about to start looking for her when she suddenly returned. "I had trouble finding one big enough," she said with a grin as she showed me a knife from the kitchen.

It was massive.

"Should I stick it into the wall?" she asked with glee.

"Hold on. I thought of one more touch while you were gone." I pulled out the bandana we'd recovered from Hank's body and then held it up against the wall. "Do you think you can pierce it without stabbing my hand in the process?"

"There's only one way to find out," she said as she jammed the tip of the knife through the bandana and into the hard southern yellow pine. If she hadn't hit a seam between the boards, the knife probably would have bounced off, but somehow it managed to strike home. When Grace released the blade, it stayed perfectly in place, and we both took two steps back and examined our work.

It gave me the chills, and I was the one who'd come up with the idea in the first place.

"Wow, that should certainly get someone's attention," Grace said.

"Now all we have to do is ignore it until someone else discovers it," I said.

"I'm not so sure I can do that," she said. "So, did I miss anything while I was sleeping?"

"As a matter of fact, you did," I said. I really wanted to share what Georgia had told me, but I'd made her a promise, and I was bound by my word to keep it.

"Well, don't hold out on me. Spill."

"All I can really say is that if one of my witnesses is telling the truth, there's a chance that Nicole isn't as free of blame as she's been leading us to believe. Whoever tried to push her over the edge may have had plenty of reason to do it."

"What do you mean?" Grace asked. "Suzanne, did you promise someone not to tell me what you learned?"

"I'm sorry. It was the only way I could get her to talk to me." I was safe using the female pronoun, since Grace and I knew that only the women had survived this trip so far.

"I get it, but that kind of puts us in an awkward position, don't you think?"

"What could I do?"

Grace thought about it for a moment, and then she said, "Tell me everything that you can, without breaking any confidences."

"That's the problem. I already did. Suffice it to say that if my source is telling the truth, which to be honest with you, I'm not sure about at all, then there was more happening behind the scenes than we were aware of."

"Well, that's cryptic enough," Grace answered. "So all we really know now that we didn't know before is that Nicole may have actually done the same thing that Georgia and Janelle tried to do. Georgia's your source, isn't she?"

"I can't say."

"You don't have to," Grace said with a smile. "After all, you two just worked a shift together before you woke me. It had to be her. Suzanne, I wouldn't believe anything that woman told me if I were you. She's most likely just trying to muddy the waters so we can't see what she's really up to."

"Do you really think that's what's happening?" I asked her.

"Trust me. She never expected you to keep your promise to her not to tell me. In fact, I'm guessing that she was counting on you running straight to me with all of the juicy details. She's the kind of woman who would rather lie, even when the truth would suit her better."

"Okay. Now I'm more confused than ever."

"So then, it's mission accomplished for her."

It was still dark out, and we'd done everything I'd felt safe doing while everyone else was sleeping so close by. "What should we do now?" Grace whispered. "There's really not much need to stand such a vigilant guard, since we know for a fact exactly where Hank is right now."

"Maybe so, but we can't give the killer another shot at Nicole."

"True. How about if we sit over by the fire and at least get warm? I swear, it's getting colder in here by the minute."

I looked over and saw that the fire was indeed beginning to die down. Walking over to it, I placed a few more logs on it, and then I took the poker and stirred up the ashes a little. Hefting the iron piece in my hand, I realized that it might make a decent weapon, certainly better than the ancient golf club I'd grabbed before.

Grace and I sat on the couch where I'd slept, spending the

time in a little whispered conversation but mostly comfortable silence. I didn't know if it was the warmth of the fire or because of the time I'd spent awake, but I suddenly awoke with a start as daylight crept in and touched my cheek.

I glanced over at Grace and saw that she'd nodded off as well.

So much for serving guard duty.

We'd both managed to fall asleep.

I just hoped that nobody had suffered because of our negligence.

CHAPTER 22

"**G**RACE, WAKE UP," I SAID for the second time that morning.

"I must have fallen asleep. Sorry. At least *you* were awake." She must have read something in my expression. "Suzanne, tell me you that didn't fall asleep, too."

"I wish I could, but I dozed off myself."

Grace stood suddenly, alarmed by my admission. We moved from person to person, not being satisfied until we saw signs that everyone under our care was still breathing.

It looked as though our lapse hadn't cost anyone their lives, which was a massive relief.

Celia was the last person we checked, and even as were confirming that she was still alive, her eyes opened and she saw us both looming over her. "What's wrong? Did something happen to Nicole?"

"No, she's fast asleep," I said, pointing in her direction farthest from the fire. "Did you still want to make breakfast, or would you like me to do it?"

"I'm happy to cook," Celia said, standing and stretching a little. "We have a problem, though."

"What's that?" I asked her.

"I'm not supposed to go into the kitchen alone, but there needs to be two people out here guarding the others. How do we manage that?"

"I'll go with you," Janelle said. "I'm awake, and I'd be happy to lend a hand. I make breakfast for my kids just about every morning before school. It's kind of a ritual for us."

"Fine. We'd better get started, then," Celia answered.

After the two women went off to the kitchen to get to work, I had a nagging feeling that something had happened while Grace and I had nodded off.

"Stay right here," I said as I decided to check on the hall mirror message we'd left.

"Suzanne, there is no way that you're going anywhere on your own, even to the bathroom."

"What about them?" I asked.

"They're on their own, as far as I'm concerned. It's about time everybody else got up anyway."

"Okay. Come on then."

"Where are we going?"

"To check on our handiwork," I said.

Only when we got to the mirror, everything we'd done earlier had vanished: the message, the bandana, and even the knife.

Someone had taken advantage of our negligence and had carefully removed all evidence of what we'd tried to do.

The question in my mind: was that a good thing or a bad one?

"What happened?" Grace asked me as she stared at the mirror.

"Someone must have done it while we nodded off," I said. I studied the mirror and saw a few smudges from the lipstick writing, but to the casual observer, there was no sign of anything that we'd done. I rubbed my finger where the knife blade had stuck into the wall, but it was hard to even see where it had bitten into the wood. Whoever had removed the traces of our work had done a pretty thorough job of it.

"Who would do this, Suzanne?"

"It had to be the actual killer, don't you think? Why else

would she want to keep the rest of us in the dark? As far as she knows, Hank is still alive and stalking her. Alarming the rest of us wouldn't do her any good."

"So we're looking for the person who took away our warning," Grace said. "That's not going to be easy, is it?"

"Has anything been that way so far?"

"No, you've got a point. I'm not sure how we proceed from here on out."

"It's pretty simple, actually," I said. "We just keep our eyes and ears open and hope the killer slips up somehow. At least Nicole didn't see our warning. I've been worried ever since we did it that she might be upset by the fact that someone left us all a reminder that they weren't finished with trying to get rid of her yet."

"I guess that goes in the silver lining department," Grace said.

"Are you two ready to eat?" Nicole asked us as she approached us. "Celia and Janelle say breakfast is ready." She leaned forward and checked her lipstick in the mirror, and I was relieved to see that at least we hadn't added to her stress level. "I can't wait to take a shower again. Last night was the first time in forever that I didn't do a deep cleaning scrub after taking off my makeup. I even got some on my pillow and a little on my sleeve. We're practically living like animals. I wonder how long we'll be stranded here."

"Surely they'll come get us today," I said, trying to sound positive.

She looked hopeful at the thought. "Really? That would be marvelous." Nicole glanced toward the stairs leading up to the second floor. "I can't believe Hank is still hiding somewhere in the lodge. When do you think he'll show himself?"

"As soon as someone rescues us, I'll bet we see him," Grace said.

"I hope so. We have some things to talk about, that's for

sure," Nicole said. "I'm beginning to realize that I was a little too cavalier with his feelings, and I want to apologize for the way I've been acting. I hope he takes me back. The more I think about it, Hank might just be the love of my life."

I didn't have the heart to tell her that particular opportunity was gone forever. Things were bad enough without her discovering that the last conversation she'd had with her former boyfriend would be that indeed, the last one she'd ever have.

Georgia popped into the hallway. "What's going on out here?"

"We're just chatting," I said.

She looked at me with alarm in her eyes. "About what?"

"Hank," Nicole said. "We're wondering when he's going to show himself."

"Maybe when he gets hungry enough, he'll pop up," Georgia said, clearly relieved that I hadn't betrayed her trust after all. "Speaking of food, Celia won't let the rest of us eat until you three join us, so let's go."

"We're coming," I said, and all four of us made our way to the kitchen.

I found it interesting that Georgia hadn't glanced at the mirror even once. Was she overcompensating trying to hide what she'd done earlier, or was it a simple oversight? I honestly couldn't tell.

The pancakes were delicious, better than I could have made myself. After eating my third one, I asked, "How did you make those taste so wonderful?"

"Hunger is a pretty good sauce," Celia said, clearly pleased with my praise.

"It was more than that, Sis," Nicole said. "I must admit that I'm impressed, too."

"I'm glad you all like them," she said.

I took another bite. "There's definitely cinnamon there, and some nutmeg as well. But there's something I'm missing. Could it be allspice?"

Celia grinned. "Wow, you really have a sophisticated palate, don't you?"

"I make donuts for a living, remember? I know my way around the spice rack. Would you care to share your recipe with me?"

"I'd be happy to," Celia answered. "Are there any volunteers for doing the dishes?"

"Why don't we let them wait?" Nicole asked. "Suzanne believes that we're going to be rescued soon, and I want to make sure Hank is okay before someone else comes along. I don't know why, but I've got a feeling that he's somewhere on the grounds, too hurt to join us. It's the only thing that makes any sense. If he could, I just know that he'd be down here with us right now. Does anyone have any objections to conducting another search?"

"I suppose it will give us something to do while we wait to be rescued," Dina said.

"Why not?" Janelle replied.

I wasn't all that excited about looking for someone I knew couldn't possibly be there, but I couldn't exactly say that out loud without tipping my hand. "Let's do it. Grace and I will take this floor."

"Actually, I think we might be better off looking in different places than we did last time."

"Honestly, Nicole, there are only so many areas someone can hide in," Georgia said.

"I suppose you're right. If there are no objections, I'll assign the teams this time. Dina, why don't you, Janelle, and Georgia start in the attic and work your way down to this floor? Suzanne, you and Grace can check the basement this time, while Celia and I explore the cottages outside. I'd like some time with my sister, if no one minds."

I could hardly object to that, and apparently neither could Celia. "That sounds good," I said.

"Then let's get busy. Remember, call out if you find anything."

"So, to the basement?" Grace asked me once the other groups went about their routes.

"Sure. At least it shouldn't take us long."

I headed for the door, with Grace on my heels.

We were two steps down the stairs when I heard the door suddenly close behind us.

I went back to check to be sure that it hadn't been by accident.

When I tried the doorknob, it was locked, and as I called out for help, I heard something heavy being pushed in front of the door.

Someone had trapped us in the basement.

While I didn't have a clue who might have done it, or more importantly, why, I realized that things must be coming to a head sooner than I'd expected.

One of our party was trying to take Grace and me out of the equation.

That wasn't going to happen, though, not if we could help it.

CHAPTER 23

"WHAT JUST HAPPENED, SUZANNE?" GRACE asked me as she joined me at the top of the stairs.

"Someone's locked us down here," I said, frantically trying to open the door.

It wouldn't budge, and even if it did, we'd still have that heavy object placed on the other side to contend with.

"There's no use fighting it," Grace said as she raced down the steps.

"You're not just giving up, are you?"

"You know me better than that," she replied. "Whoever tried to keep us down here must not know about the cellar door."

"There's another way out of here?" I asked as I followed her lead.

"Janelle mentioned it to me yesterday. I thought you heard it, too."

"No, I must have missed it."

"Her team found it when they were searching down here yesterday," Grace explained.

"Did they all know about it?" I asked as Grace worked at unlocking the barrel latch of the other exit. It appeared to have been neglected for years, and it was going to take a little work to get it open.

"Absolutely," Grace said as she continued to fiddle with the latch.

I found a hammer on a nearby workbench and said, "Step aside."

"Do we really need to break it?" Grace asked me.

"We do when someone's life is at stake," I said, taking the claw end of the hammer, putting it under the latch, and lifting abruptly, snapping it off. A little bit of wood splintered when I did it, but the door would at least open now.

"Suzanne, what do you know that I don't?" she asked me. I held onto the hammer. It just might be useful again.

"Think about it," I said as we raced outside. "Dina, Georgia, and Janelle all knew about this other exit. That means that none of them would have tried to lock us down here."

"Did we just eliminate three suspects?" Grace asked me.

"As a matter of fact, that's exactly what happened. We know for a fact that Hank didn't do anything, so that just leaves Celia and Nicole."

"Then it's got to be Celia who's been trying to get rid of her sister," Grace said.

"I don't think so," I answered as we raced toward the cottages.

"Are you saying that Nicole tried to push herself off the edge of the cliff? That doesn't make any sense at all."

"*Nobody* tried to push her, just like nobody tried to run her over earlier or blew out her pilot light," I said. "She's been setting us up from the very start. Georgia told me that Hank was going to fire Nicole, and she couldn't have that, so she must have pushed him off the edge herself to keep that from happening. I'm willing to bet that Nicole couldn't stand the idea of losing her job to one of you, but the money she'd be losing was even more important to her. You said yourself that she only buys the best, and I believe you. I've seen her outfits and jewelry with my own eyes, and after Dina lost so much of Nicole's money playing the stock market, what's the only other source of income she's had access to?"

"Celia's trust fund," Grace said breathlessly. "*That's* why she wanted to extend the arrangement. If she's forced to turn the money over to her sister next week, then Celia and everyone else will know that Nicole has been stealing from her."

"I'm willing to bet the books won't stand up to a careful audit. She even explained something away that we noticed earlier. When she wiped that warning off the mirror, she got a little lipstick on her sleeve. Did you see how quickly she explained it away? The woman's a gifted liar, I'll give her that much. She even set up something to make me sympathetic to her cause by booby-trapping her own door. Nicole's been playing us for fools from the very beginning."

"Let me get this straight. You're saying that my boss was never anyone's target at all? You're right! That explains why Celia had to go, and so did Hank! Suzanne, are we too late to save her?"

"I don't know, but we have to at least try," I said as we hurried to the exact spot where Hank had met his own fate.

As we neared Hemlock cottage, Grace asked me, "What about those footprints in the snow we found?"

"Nicole had to be sure that Hank was really dead," I said. "I don't think she bought our story from the beginning. I wonder if she spotted his body, even though we couldn't. I saw a dark impression, but I couldn't be sure it was Hank. Maybe she could, though. That's the only way that any of this makes sense, given the way she's been acting."

They weren't in Hemlock or Fir or Spruce.

As we approached Pine, the last cottage in the row, I realized that Celia had just about run out of time when I looked in through the window and saw Nicole and her both inside. Nicole's hand was reaching into her sweatshirt pocket, and Celia's back was turned to her.

Whatever was about to occur was going to happen quickly, and there wasn't anything we could do about it.

That wasn't going to stop me from trying, though, as I watched Nicole pull a handgun out of her sweatshirt and turn it toward her sister.

CHAPTER 24

"NICOLE!" I SCREAMED AT THE top of my lungs just as I swung the hammer in my hand back and threw it through the glass window. The pane shattered on impact, but we couldn't afford to wait around to see what happened after that. I grabbed Grace's arm. "Run!"

She nodded, and we both took off, I assumed heading for the others at the lodge. I glanced back and saw Celia bolting into the bathroom and slamming the door behind her! Those doors were made from heavy wood, and I hoped that they'd stop the bullets, but I couldn't be too concerned about that now. I'd reacted to the scene about to play out without giving much thought to what might happen next. Would Nicole follow us, or would she finish the job she'd intended to do by killing Celia first? I heard an explosion behind us, and I could swear that I felt the slug whistle through the air past my ear. She'd made her choice. Evidently we were a more active threat to her plans.

I glanced over at Grace, who had peeled away and was running in a completely different direction than I'd been. Instead of heading toward the lodge, she was pointed directly for the maze. "Where are you going?" I shouted out.

"The maze," she said as she pointed in that direction.

"Why?"

"It's safer there!" she said breathlessly.

I didn't agree with her, but I didn't really have any choice at that point. I changed my direction, intent on catching up with her by the time she got to the entrance. It might not have been the best place to run away from her assassin boss, but I was going wherever Grace was heading.

I took a second and turned to look back at Nicole. She was standing in place, holding the handgun carefully and pointing it straight at me.

This was it.

As close as I'd come in the past to being killed, my luck had finally run out.

And then I heard the hammer click.

Instead of shooting a round at us, it had been a misfire.

There was time to save ourselves, and I was about to tell Grace not to go into the maze when she vanished inside.

I managed to come up with a burst of momentary speed, and a few seconds later, I was inside as well. Just as I left the outside behind, I glanced back one last time.

Nicole still had the gun in her hands, but now she was running, too. She was going to chase us down and shoot us, and there wasn't a thing we could do about it.

I'd used my only weapon to try to save Celia, and it might just end up costing Grace and me our lives.

"What do we do now?" Grace asked me breathlessly, sobbing as she hurried along the maze.

"We keep going and hope for the best," I said as I caught up with her.

"You go on ahead," she said as she collapsed to the ground. "Suzanne, I got us into this. You go. I'll try to stop her."

"That's not happening. Either we get out of this together or we die side by side," I said.

"How touching," Nicole said as she rounded the corner,

holding the handgun out toward us. "I choose the second option, if it's all the same to you."

Running into the maze had indeed been a fatal mistake, and our final one.

CHAPTER 25

"WHY ARE YOU DOING THIS?" Grace asked her as I dropped to the ground beside my best friend at Nicole's coaxing. "I thought we were friends."

"Do you honestly think that I want to shoot you both?" Nicole asked her incredulously. "If you hadn't been snooping around so much, none of this had to happen. Honestly, I didn't think either one of you were any good at this detecting business. I figured I'd get you both up here, throw around some false clues, and you'd end up backing up my story when the police finally showed up. Now I've got to kill you both, and then I have to take care of that pesky sister of mine."

"At least tell us one thing," I said. "It was all about the money, wasn't it?"

"Of course it was! Why should Celia get any, when I knew that she'd just squander it? I started borrowing a little from her trust when Dina lost my money, but it was so easy that I couldn't stop myself. It would have been bad enough to lose out on Celia's money, but then Hank said that he was going to fire me! I should really kill Georgia, too, while I'm at it. She's the one who started this whole mess."

This woman was a sociopath! If anybody escaped her wrath, it would be a miracle, all for pretty things and nice clothes!

I had to stall her. Maybe Celia would go for help once she

knew that she wasn't the target anymore, at least not the main one. "Where did you get the gun?"

"I'm not going to stand here answering your questions," Nicole said with disgust.

"You hid it upstairs and grabbed it this morning, didn't you? That's why you waited until Celia went to the bathroom. Why didn't you go ahead and shoot her then?"

"Because you wouldn't go to sleep, you fool! I was going to blame it on Hank, but I didn't get the chance."

"He's dead, though," I said.

"I know that. I saw his body where he crawled under that tree, at least part of it. You left the message on the mirror for me, didn't you?"

Maybe I still had a bluff left in me. "Message? What are you talking about?"

Nicole wasn't buying it. "Don't kid a kidder. It was the two of you. Is that what gave me away, that lipstick on my sleeve? You saw that, didn't you?"

I nodded. This was hopeless. It was clear that Nicole was nearly out of patience with us.

I had one chance left. If I could lunge out at her, then maybe Grace could get the weapon if I managed to dislodge it somehow. I would most likely die, but she'd at least have a fighting chance. Then again, maybe we'd get lucky and the gun would misfire again.

I shot out from my hands and feet, and just at that moment, as though we'd timed it perfectly, Grace was just a single beat behind me.

We still might have died if Celia hadn't come around the corner at that moment swinging a heavy branch at her sister's head. She screamed a horrific war cry just as Grace and I got to Nicole. If the cold-blooded killer hadn't begun to turn toward her sister, one of us would have probably been dead, but it had been enough of a distraction to take the gun off us for a moment, and that was all we needed.

As Grace and I hit her legs nearly simultaneously, I could feel the impact of Celia's branch on Nicole's body. She fell on top of Grace and me, and for a moment I thought one of us still might get shot, but I soon realized that Nicole wasn't in any shape to kill anyone else; she was unconscious.

Celia had aimed for her sister's head, and it had evidently been a direct hit.

"Are you two okay?" Celia asked, her voice shaking as she stared down at her sister. "Did I kill her?"

I checked for a pulse and found one immediately. "You managed to knock her out, but she's still alive. Does anyone have anything we can tie her hands with?"

"Why don't we use her fancy belt?" Grace suggested. "It must have cost her a fortune, so it's only fitting, right?"

I did as she suggested, and then Grace said, "We couldn't have planned that better if we'd tried."

"Sometimes quick action is better than a well-thought-out plan," I said.

"Should we just leave her here?" Celia asked.

"Not on your life," I said. "I don't care if we have her gun *and* she's unconscious. I will never turn my back on your sister again."

"Smart thinking," Celia said. "Neither will I."

With Nicole's hands bound, I grabbed one leg and Grace grabbed the other. We dragged the killer out of the maze and into the lawn in front of it, no doubt ruining her precious outfit in the process.

I couldn't have cared less.

CHAPTER 26

"**S**UZANNE, ARE YOU ALL RIGHT?" a familiar voice asked me as my husband rushed into the lodge searching frantically for me.

"Jake, what are you doing here?" I couldn't have been happier to see him!

"Are you kidding? Stephen and I have been going crazy trying to get to you both." At that moment, he noticed Nicole in the corner, bound and now gagged as well. "What's going on, Suzanne? Have you gotten yourself into some trouble again?"

What an understatement. "Nothing that we couldn't handle." I thought it had been fitting that we'd used Hank's bandana to silence Nicole once she came to. I had no idea that woman had even heard all of the words she used in describing us all. The others had clearly been surprised by Nicole's actions over the weekend, though Georgia had claimed that she'd known it all along.

After we'd captured and secured her, we'd waited for someone to come, since there was nothing else to be done, but it was a really pleasant surprise knowing that Jake and Stephen had been the ones to show up first.

After Jake and Stephen were brought up to date on what had happened during our time at the lodge, Officer Grant went off to use his radio to call it in, but not without taking Grace with him first. "The road up here took forever to cross. Part of it was nearly washed out, but we made it anyway," Jake explained.

"I'm so happy to see you," I said, allowing myself to be folded up into his arms.

"Hey, I thought you were finished with amateur sleuthing," he whispered softly in my ear.

"I thought so, too, but it turns out that I was wrong. I just can't seem to help myself."

"And killers everywhere are quaking in their boots because of it. Are you ready to go home? It won't be right away, because there will be statements to make, but we should be able to get back home by tonight."

"I can't wait," I said. "I missed you," I added.

"But you didn't need me," he said with a grin as he pulled away from me.

"Always, now and forever."

I'd meant what I'd said, too. I had honestly believed that I was finished with tracking down killers, but I realized that if the right circumstances ever came along again, I wouldn't hesitate.

It was too important, and I couldn't just turn my back on it.

I just hoped that it didn't happen again anytime soon.

After all, I still had a vacation coming to me, at least as far as I was concerned.

RECIPES

SUZANNE'S BASIC DONUT RECIPE SHE USES AT THE LODGE

This one has changed a little since I first made it, so I thought I'd do a follow-up on it for you all. I like tweaking old familiar recipes, and just as Suzanne does, I'm constantly trying new ingredients in search of the perfect donut. I haven't found it yet, but it doesn't mean that I don't have fun searching for it.

Ingredients

- 7 to 8 cups bread flour (holding one out in reserve)
- 2 cups granulated sugar
- 2 teaspoons baking soda
- 2 teaspoons nutmeg
- 2 teaspoons cinnamon
- 4 dashes of salt
- 1 cup sour cream
- 2 eggs, beaten
- 2 cups milk
- 8 cups oil for frying (I like canola or peanut oil for this)

Directions

The directions are fairly simple to follow. Heat enough oil

to fry your donuts to 375 degrees F. While the oil is heating, combine the flour, sugar, baking soda, nutmeg, cinnamon, and salt in a large mixing bowl and sift it all together. Add the two lightly beaten eggs to the dry mix, then add the sour cream and the milk, stirring it all in lightly. If needed, use more milk or flour to get the dough to a workable mix. It shouldn't stick to your hands when you touch it, but it should be moist enough to remain flexible. Knead this mix lightly, then roll it out to about 1/4 of an inch thickness. Using your donut hole cutter or two different-sized glasses of the diameters you'd like, press the donut shapes out, reserving the holes for a later frying.

When the oil is ready, put four to six donuts in the pot.

Let the donuts cook for approximately 2 minutes on one side, then check them. If they are golden brown on one side, flip them over with a large chopstick or wooden skewer, and let those sides cook another 2 minutes.

Once the donuts are finished, remove them to a cooling rack and be sure to drain them thoroughly before serving. Try a simple icing using vanilla extract, confectioner's sugar, and a little water until you have a fine slurry, and then coat them.

Serves 6 to 10 depending on the size glasses you use.

GLAZED YEAST DONUTS THAT REQUIRE RAISING

There are three basic kinds of donuts we make at home: easy rolled out, raised, and cake. To add to the mix, some are fried in oil, while other healthier versions bake in the oven, but no matter what kind of donuts you make, these homemade treats are sure to be a hit!

Ingredients

- 1 cup milk (whole or 2%), scalded
- 3/4 cup granulated sugar
- 1/8 teaspoon table salt
- 5 to 6 cups flour, all purpose
- 2 teaspoons cinnamon
- 1 teaspoon nutmeg
- Active dry yeast, 1 packet (1/4 ounce)
- 1/2 cup water, warm but not hot
- 1/2 cup butter (margarine can be substituted)
- 2 eggs, lightly beaten
- 8 cups oil for frying; canola or peanut are my favorite

Directions

First, scald the milk (see directions in any good cookbook), then stir in the sugar and salt until everything is dissolved. Let this mixture cool, and in the meantime, in another bowl, add 3 cups of the flour, cinnamon, and nutmeg together, holding the rest for later, including 1/2 cup of flour back for flouring the cutting surface when the donut rounds are cut out. When the liquid is cool to the touch, add the mixed dry ingredients slowly, stirring to make sure there aren't any clumps. In yet another bowl, dissolve the yeast in warm water, not hot, then stir in the milk-and-flour mixture, and finally, the melted butter or margarine and the beaten eggs. Add the remaining flour to the mix slowly, 1/2 cup at a time, until the dough is firm to the touch and bounces back slightly when touched. Spray another bowl with cooking spray, add the ball of dough, and cover for 30 minutes to allow it to rise. Then turn the dough out onto a floured surface, using the flour you reserved earlier, and roll it out until it's anywhere from 1/4 to 1/2 inch thick. Cut out your donut shapes, put them on floured baking sheets, cover, and let rise for another 30 minutes. While the dough is resting for the second time, heat the oil until it reaches 375 degrees F. Carefully add the rounds and holes to the oil, a few at a time, turning after 2 minutes on each side to cook thoroughly. Remove, drain on a cooling rack, and then glaze or sprinkle with powdered sugar and serve.

This recipe serves 4 to 6 people, depending on the size of your donuts.

SUZANNE'S FAVORITE SMALL APPLE FRITTER BITES

Given the way Suzanne and Grace share fritters at the beginning of the book, how can we not offer these here? They are delightful little morsels, whether they are coated with icing, powdered sugar, or the topping of your choice. I like them best when they're warm, since I rarely get the chance to eat them cool. That's how fast they fly out of my kitchen!

Ingredients

- 1 cup all-purpose flour
- 1/3 cup granulated sugar
- 1 tablespoon baking powder
- 1 tablespoon cinnamon
- 1/4 teaspoon salt
- 1/3 cup milk (2% or whole)
- 1 egg, beaten
- 2/3 cup chopped apple (something tart, like Granny Smith)
- 8 cups oil for cooking (we like canola or peanut)

Directions

While your oil is heating in a large pot to 375 degrees F, mix the flour, sugar, baking powder, cinnamon, and salt in a large mixing bowl. Sift this mixture into another bowl, and then stir in the milk and beaten egg. When you have a nice batter consistency, coat the apple pieces lightly with flour, and then fold them into the batter. Using two teaspoons, scoop up the batter and push it into the oil with the second teaspoon, being careful not to splash the oil. After 2 minutes, flip the small fritter bites and allow them to cook on the other side for an additional 2 minutes. Take them out when they're done, and coat them with powdered sugar, icing, or even apple butter if you're feeling particularly adventurous.

Serves 2 to 4 people

If you enjoy Jessica Beck Mysteries and you would like to be notified when the next book is being released, please send your email address to newreleases@jessicabeckmysteries.net. Your email address will not be shared, sold, bartered, traded, broadcast, or disclosed in any way. There will be no spam from us, just a friendly reminder when the latest book is being released.

Also, be sure to visit our website at jessicabeckmysteries.net for valuable information about Jessica's books.

OTHER BOOKS BY JESSICA BECK

Made in the USA
Middletown, DE
02 October 2015